BRONTE
TEMPESTRA
AND THE
L/GHTNING STEEDS

BRONTE TEMPESTRA

AND THE
LIGHTNING STEEDS

BEX HOGAN
Illustrated by Hannah McCaffery

Piccadilly
PRESS

First published in Great Britain in 2024 by
PICCADILLY PRESS
4th Floor, Victoria House, Bloomsbury Square
London WC1B 4DA
Owned by Bonnier Books
Sveavägen 56, Stockholm, Sweden
bonnierbooks.co.uk/PiccadillyPress

A CIP catalogue record for this book is available from the British Library.

ISBN: 978-1-80078-469-7
Also available as an ebook and in audio

1

Typeset by Emily Bornoff
Printed and bound in Great Britain by Clays Ltd, Elcograf S.p.A.

Piccadilly Press is an imprint of Bonnier Books UK
bonnierbooks.co.uk

For Odi – always follow your dreams x

BH

For my Mum & Dad x

HMcC

ANCIENT RUINS

THE OLD FOREST

OAK

CHERRY

WEAPON TRAINING HALL

HEADMASTER'S TOWER

RIDING ARENA

AINING OUNDS

TRAINING GROUNDS

TOURNAMENT ARENA

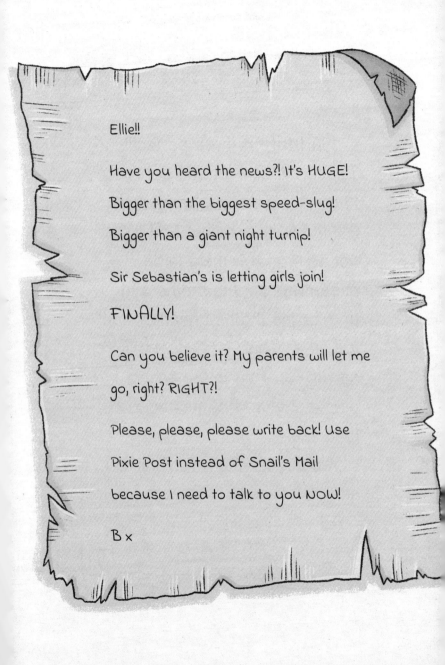

Ellie!!

Have you heard the news?! It's HUGE!
Bigger than the biggest speed-slug!
Bigger than a giant night turnip!

Sir Sebastian's is letting girls join!

FINALLY!

Can you believe it? My parents will let me

go, right? RIGHT?!

Please, please, please write back! Use

Pixie Post instead of Snail's Mail

because I need to talk to you NOW!

B x

WAHHHH! B, that's perfect!! I'm sure they'll let you go! They know how much you've always wanted to be a knight, and it's not as if you're likely to be queen with six big brothers in line for the throne ahead of you! We all saw how perfect you were as Sir Pen Tine in the school play last year! Let me know what they say.

Are you having a fun summer so far?

El x

Summer Holiday Diary, Day 17

Super stormy day, even for the Storm Kingdom! The hailstones were big enough to play smash-ball with, and Barak and I got soaked catching them! Mum wasn't too impressed at the state of us. She threatened to take me dress shopping tomorrow. But I told her that I couldn't because Gale has been making new lightning beat-sticks, and we were planning to catch stray bolts. I'm not sure she thought that was a good excuse. And then the day after there's a jousting display and I know she wouldn't make me miss that. Hope the knights don't get blown off their battle boars!

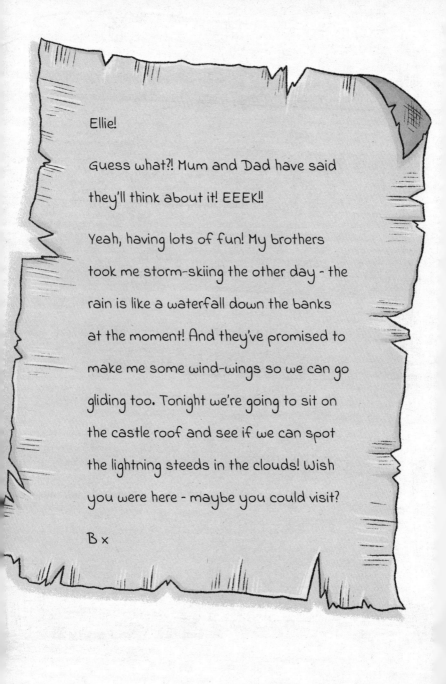

Ellie!

Guess what?! Mum and Dad have said they'll think about it! EEEK!!

Yeah, having lots of fun! My brothers took me storm-skiing the other day - the rain is like a waterfall down the banks at the moment! And they've promised to make me some wind-wings so we can go gliding too. Tonight we're going to sit on the castle roof and see if we can spot the lightning steeds in the clouds! Wish you were here - maybe you could visit?

B x

Summer Holiday Diary, Day 22

Last night I stayed up REALLY late with my brothers watching for lightning steeds. We had lots of fun, but no luck spotting them — or the thunder trolls. Bolt says he saw the steeds once years ago, but I think he's just making that up. Flash says that you're more likely to see them when they come to ground, and that's super rare. But they do leave scorch marks behind and Dad says he's seen them before! I'm so jealous — I'd LOVE to see even their hoof-prints! Maybe one day! We'll keep looking though — we might spot a flash of black and orange in the sky eventually. I'm not so bothered that we didn't see the thunder trolls. Not with the noise they make!

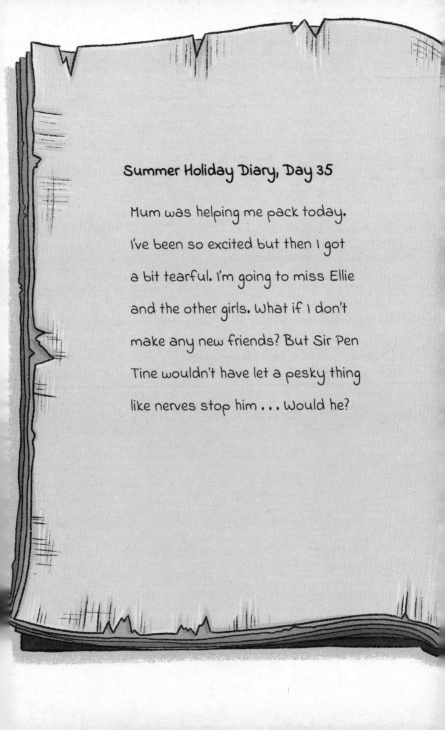

Summer Holiday Diary, Day 35

Mum was helping me pack today.
I've been so excited but then I got
a bit tearful. I'm going to miss Ellie
and the other girls. What if I don't
make any new friends? But Sir Pen
Tine wouldn't have let a pesky thing
like nerves stop him ... Would he?

Troll Trouble

Bronte Tempestra leaned out of the carriage as it frantically bumped along the cobbles. She brushed away the hair whipping across her face and screamed.

'Turn right, Hopper! NOW!'

The vehicle lurched sharply, moving just before a gigantic foot smashed onto the ground. **THWOMP!**

Bronte gasped. 'That was *way* too close.'

'Hold on tight!' Hopper, the driver, called back, as he fought to keep control of the speed-slugs tugging on the reins.

This was *not* how things were supposed to be. Yes, it was true that a journey through the Storm Kingdom was always an experience, with the torrential rain and gusty winds shaking the carriage like a snow globe. But Bronte was used to that. This . . . this was something else.

Thunder trolls were falling from the sky!

Actual enormous thunder trolls, who were supposed to live *above* the clouds, were dropping down like monstrous rain, causing the world to shake each time one hit the ground.

The trolls seemed as confused as Bronte was and stumbled about so that the carriage had to swerve and dodge its way past their clumsy – and lethal – feet.

This was a disaster! Thunder trolls and humans did *not* belong together!

The thunder trolls didn't look at all like Bronte had imagined they would either. Whenever she'd gazed into the sky, hoping to catch a glimpse of them, she'd expected to see hairy scary monsters leaping about. But there was nothing hairy about these trolls. At first glance Bronte thought they were made of stone, but then she realised it was cloud. They were far from floaty though – they were horribly solid.

'Incoming!' Hopper shouted, pulling the speed-slugs to a sudden halt.

Bronte braced herself, just as a vast tree landed with a thump in front of them. She gulped.

'Hang on,' Hopper warned her, before they set off again at high speed.

Bronte watched in horror as the thunder trolls plucked more trees from the Fundry Forest, like they were nothing more than hairs from an ogre's chin, and tossed them aside, oblivious to the destruction.

'What are they doing down here?' Bronte cried. How had they managed to escape the lightning steeds? The blazing horses were the only ones who could handle the trolls, keeping them running on top of the clouds and preventing them from doing . . . this!

'Haven't you noticed?' Hopper yelled above the chaos. 'No lightning!'

He was right! How hadn't she noticed that the lightning that usually illuminated the skies day and night was gone?

What was going on? Where were the lightning steeds? The trolls had only been here moments and they were already destroying everything in their path. What if they trampled through the crop fields? Or suppose they destroyed the buffer trees that protected the villages from the worst of the storms? Or even worse, what if the trolls *squished* the villages?

It was hard to believe that only yesterday, when Bronte had set off on her journey, all had been fine. Better than fine – she was living her dream! As Hopper had loaded her trunk, Bronte's mum and dad – Queen Mira and King Roy of the Storm Kingdom – had given her a big hug. They had been as nervous and excited as she was. New term, new year . . . new school. Her mum had kept saying that if Bronte didn't like it, if it wasn't all she'd imagined it would be, then she could go back to her old school any time, but why the curly custard would Bronte leave? Training to become a knight was all she had ever wanted . . .

BUMP! The carriage flew into the air so suddenly that Bronte hit her head on the roof. She clutched her much-loved knitted knight toy close to her chest.

'Sorry!' Hopper shouted. 'Debris in the road!'

Catching her breath, Bronte dared to peer out of the window again and was relieved to see the thunder trolls were now falling behind. *Phew!*

She looked up to the sky, all black and stormy but strangely empty without the flashes of light. It was worrying. Where the green gravy *were* the lightning steeds? Surely they would come to the rescue soon?

Sleepily Bronte closed her eyes. She imagined the powerful creatures swooping down to her carriage to take her with them. Just think! How amazing would it be to ride one of the magnificent lightning horses, its black coat flecked with fiery reds and oranges. She could see herself now – galloping across the land, sword in hand, rounding up the troublesome trolls before chasing them back into the sky, the clouds catching in her hair as they sped along. Together with the steeds, she would save everyone from the trolls' havoc, and across the kingdom they would applaud her for saving the day, chanting her name over and over!

Bronte! Bronte! Bronte . . .

Sir Sebastian's School for Squires

'We're nearly there, miss.'

Hopper's voice woke Bronte so abruptly that she clonked her head on the window. Rubbing it better, she took in her surroundings.

The journey had taken over a week – south through the Storm Kingdom, then down through the Mist Queendom and into the Heart of the Kingdoms – and since that one terrifying day, there had been no sign of the thunder trolls. Bronte had sent an urgent letter to her parents via Pixie Post, but Hopper had pointed out she wouldn't receive a reply while she was travelling.

'I'm sure those trolls will already be back in the sky,' he'd said to reassure her. 'Your family will have fixed things, mark my words.'

It *had* eased Bronte's concerns slightly, and in any case, she had no choice but to wait to find out what the green gravy had happened. But right now, she had other things on her mind.

The road they were on was unfamiliar. Normally they would have turned left at the grizzly-goat bridge to head east towards her old school in the Realm of Education, but not today. The closer she got to her destination, the more nervous she became.

All Bronte had ever wanted was to be a

knight – riding one of the legendary battle boars, dressed in shining armour, with a sword gleaming in her hand and a firecat at her side. She'd dreamed of dramatic rescues, of honour and chivalry. But there had always been one big problem – the knight school hadn't let girls attend.

Until now.

That summer, Sir Sebastian's School for Squires had announced that, for the first time in its history, they were going to admit *all* children. What had happened to change their minds? Who knew. But Bronte liked to imagine it was because some ancient text foretold of a knight who would be braver and more heroic than any before. That this knight would be a girl. That this knight would be her. That she alone would –

All daydreams blew away as the carriage

turned off the main road and the school finally came into view.

Bronte had seen some castles in her time but WOW!

Four unbelievably massive trees loomed before her, positioned in an irregular square shape. Treehouses filled their branches, and between the trees were towers and turrets, all linked together by rope bridges. Colourful flowers wound up the stone walls like maypole ribbons. From the top of the towers, flags representing each of the sixteen kingdoms flapped in the wind and Bronte searched until she found hers: a grey flag with a black horse in the centre, and bolts of lightning in each corner.

Bronte's excitement flipped to panic. What if no one liked her? Or worse, what if she was a totally rubbish knight?

The carriage stopped outside the entrance and Bronte climbed out, staring up at her new school nervously.

Hopper helped unstrap her trunk and noticed she had gone quiet. 'It's not too late to change your mind,' he said. 'I could find my way to your old school blindfolded and I'm sure they'd have you back in a flash. No one would blame you for wanting to be in the Realm of Education, rather than out here in the middle of nowhere.'

Bronte looked down at her toy of Sir Pen Tine. The legendary knight was her inspiration. He wouldn't turn back now and neither would she.

'No, this is where I want to be.'

'You sure, Miss Bronte?' Hopper glanced towards the school and pulled a face. 'Just a lot of prancing about, isn't it? Reckon you can do better than that.'

Prancing?! How could he call being a hero *prancing*?!

But she didn't want to argue with him, so instead she gave the driver a big hug. 'Please be careful on the way home. Watch out for the trolls.'

'Oh, I'm not worried about them, Miss Bronte. Those trolls and the lightning steeds have never left the Storm Kingdom in the entire history of Everdale. There'll be a letter waiting for you, telling you all is back to normal, you'll see.'

Yes, Bronte thought. He was right. The grown-ups would have fixed everything.

'Anyway,' Hopper added, 'don't worry about me. You just take care of yourself.'

One last hug and he was gone.

'Come on,' Bronte whispered to herself. 'You can do this. Feet firm, head high. Be brave.'

Bronte walked to the open gates, which were

set between two tall turrets. Before her was a courtyard bustling with students. They were greeting each other with boisterous knuckle-knocking handshakes and cheerfully exchanging friendly insults.

Huh.

That was weird. Boys here. Boys there. Boys everywhere. Surely . . . ? There was no *way* she could be the *only* girl! Frantically searching about, Bronte wasn't paying attention to where she was going until –

Oof!

She was knocked back, crashing down hard onto her trunk.

Tonkins

'Is there something wrong with your eyesight, young lady?'

An old man in purple robes peered down at her from beneath bushy eyebrows that looked like two puff-snails.

'Sorry, sorry,' Bronte said, scrambling to her feet. 'I'm new.'

'A feeble excuse.'

It wasn't an excuse, thought Bronte indignantly. *It was an explanation!*

'Year One?' he continued.

'No, Year Four,' Bronte said. 'I'm nine. I'm just short.' As was her temper. She *hated* being reminded about her height – she'd had enough teasing from her brothers to last a lifetime!

He raised one of his hairy eyebrows. 'Very well. Come with me.'

'Actually, I wonder if you know whether any post has come for me? From my parents?'

The old man glared at her.

When he didn't answer, Bronte continued. 'It's very important. The thunder trolls were causing chaos and the lightning steeds were missing and –'

'Let me stop you there,' the man said. 'I have no interest in your tales, nor am I your postal service. Any letters will have been taken to your room.'

'But have you heard anything?' Bronte persisted. 'Are the kingdoms *safe*?'

'I haven't the faintest idea what you're babbling on about and nor do I care. What did you say your name was?'

But before Bronte could answer, another man came running towards them, his battered leather apron covered in muck.

'Excuse me, Sir Calliphus, we have a problem.'

'Calm yourself, Lampton,' Sir Calliphus scolded. Bronte was relieved to discover it wasn't just her he was grumpy with. 'What sort of problem?'

'Someone left the cloud shed open. Half our supply has gone.'

Bronte's ears pricked up at the mention of clouds. They must be for the battle boars! The rare beasts that the knights rode were from the Vanishing Kingdom – the rogue land that moved location at random, so no one ever knew where it could be found. You might see it drifting through the sky or floating on the ocean – and once, Bronte had heard, it had been seen balancing precariously on top of a mountain peak. Because of this, the battle boars required the most outlandish mixture of foods: seaweed, crushed ice, clouds . . .

Sir Calliphus growled. 'How hard is it to shut a door behind you?'

Lampton stared at Sir Calliphus, uncertain whether he was supposed to answer or not.

'Well, you'll simply have to catch more clouds,' Sir Calliphus said.

Lampton shuffled awkwardly. 'Several of our cloud nets are missing too, sir. I really think you should come and see.'

'Must I solve *every* problem?' Sir Calliphus cried, throwing his hands above his head. 'Right, off we go!'

While Bronte was very sad that the battle boars' food was going missing, she also didn't want to be forgotten about and so she coughed politely to remind Sir Calliphus she was there. 'What about me?'

Sir Calliphus rolled his eyes, then cast his gaze around the courtyard. 'Tonkins!' he called abruptly to a short, plump boy, wearing a ridiculous wide-brimmed hat trimmed with a red feather that clashed with his auburn curls.

The boy, Tonkins, looked surprised to be summoned and pointed to his chest mouthing, 'Me?'

'Yes, *you*. Come here,' Sir Calliphus said, exasperated.

'How may I be of service, sir?' Tonkins said, bowing low with a flourish. He looked so silly that Bronte couldn't help but smile.

'Get up and stop that ridiculousness,' Sir Calliphus sighed, which Bronte thought was a bit hypocritical considering his own melodramatic display moments ago. 'You're in Year Four, are you not? Please show your new classmate where to go.'

Before Tonkins could reply, Sir Calliphus swept off, leaving Bronte with her guide. The boy looked at her with a cheerful face and smiling eyes.

'Hi, I'm Sammy,' he said, stretching his hand out. 'But you can call me Tonkins. I mean, it's my surname. It's not like some random name or anything. That would be weird. It's just what everyone calls me. Apart from Lance – have you met Lance? He calls me Snotkins. Please don't call me that. Hey, your hair is so cool, I love that blue bit … er …' He paused for breath, as if only just realising he had no idea who he was actually talking to.

'I'm Bronte.' Bronte rescued him, self-consciously stroking the top of the pale blue streak that blazed like lightning through her dark hair. 'And thanks. I've always had it. Think it's a family thing.'

'Here, let me help you with your trunk,' he said, and together they grabbed the handle and pulled it along. 'You can leave it over here with the others; they'll all get taken to our cabins later.'

'Cabins?' Bronte asked, as they dumped her luggage and began to walk together through the courtyard. She'd assumed they'd be taken to one of the towers.

'Yeah, we're in the triple-trunk oak this year. Near the bottom, but it's still the best tree.'

'We get to sleep in the treehouses? Breezy!'

'Not really, you hardly notice the wind –' Tonkins began, but Bronte interrupted him.

'No, I mean "breezy" like it's a good thing. Sorry – it's a Storm Kingdom saying.'

'You're from one of the Weather Kingdoms?'

'Yep, my parents kind of rule it.' She felt a bit awkward saying that, not wanting Tonkins to treat her any differently because she was a princess.

But she needn't have worried, because he carried on as if he hadn't heard her.

'I'm from the Cactus Kingdom myself, you know, one of the Floral Kingdoms. Have you ever been there? It's all right, apart from all the pricklypods. You stand on one of those? Zowcher! My friend George once had a spike *this long* stuck in his foot.' And he held his fingers apart to suggest a length Bronte suspected was an exaggeration. 'So, you excited to be here? My uncle came here when he was younger and said it was the best time of his life, which is why I came too. He's a knight now to the Queen of the Ivy Queendom, and maybe one day I will be too. Not a queen, a knight. I hope. Not much point going to knight school if you don't end up being a knight! Bet it's a bit weird, being new in Year Four. I mean, it was weird when I was new too, but back in Year One we were *all* new so it didn't matter. But I'll tell you everything you need to know. Let's see . . . The teachers are nice, except Sir Calliphus, who you've already met. He's deputy head and a mean old sprout, but just ignore him – we all do. The headmaster, Sir Blake, is ancient. Like, honestly, he must be a thousand or something, and he never leaves his tower, so you don't have to worry about him much either.'

By the time they reached the magnificent triple-trunk oak, where a small group of boys were gathered, Bronte felt windswept by the talking tornado!

'This is our class,' Tonkins said, gesturing to the other students gathered outside at the base of the tree. There couldn't have been more than twelve of them.

'Is this everyone?' Bronte asked in surprise. 'I thought there'd be loads more.'

'Yeah, some people have left and there haven't been as many students joining these past few years. Can't understand why not. Who wouldn't want to come here –'

'And no other girls?'

Tonkins shrugged. 'Can't see any.'

The sound of someone grandly clearing his

throat made the children look up.

In the treehouse balcony, running a hand through his perfect mane of hair, was a strong-looking man wearing shiny chain mail. His moustache, which curled flamboyantly at the ends, was immaculately trimmed.

'Well, hello, young squires,' the man boomed in a voice that could only be described as heroic. 'It is I, Sir Roland Ripple. Yes, *the* Sir Roland Ripple! Also known as Sir R and R, or Sir Double R, if you will. For those of you new to the school, you probably know me best from my legendary days as poster boy for *Knights Weekly* magazine, or for my jousting record – yet to be beaten! How fortunate you are to now benefit from my wisdom.'

Bronte thought he looked more like a preening pidwigeon fluffing out his feathers than someone who could defend the people. She leaned over to Tonkins. 'Are there other new children then?' she whispered.

'No, only you,' Tonkins replied softly. 'He just likes to talk about himself.'

'Allow me to introduce a new member of staff, who shall be *assisting* me in teaching you this year,' Sir Ripple continued. 'Please give a warm welcome to Lady Flora Fennel.'

There was a gasp from the crowd as a fierce woman strode out to stand beside Sir Ripple, two swords crossed on her back. She folded her arms and raised a challenging eyebrow.

Bronte gazed in awe. But . . . how could she be a knight? Girls hadn't been allowed before. So who was she? A warrior of some kind?

'Lady Flora is a most delightful addition to our little family here at Sir Sebastian's,' Sir Ripple said, throwing his arm around her shoulder. 'And don't let the fact she's a woman fool you – she's quite the fighter, I can tell you –'

'Actually, it's Lady *Fennel*,' she said, removing Sir Ripple's arm and stepping away from him. 'And I think I can make my own introduction, thank you.' She glared so severely at Sir Ripple that Bronte could almost hear him wince. But her gaze softened as she turned to the students. 'I can't wait to get to know you all, and we're going to start straight away. We have something exciting planned.' She paused. 'But first, some of you might be wondering how I can be a knight, when the school only opened its doors to all children this year. Well, that's a mystery for you to solve. Whoever correctly guesses my story first will win a prize.'

The crowd murmured excitedly and Bronte smiled. She had just been set her first quest! There was no way she'd let anyone else win that prize – it was going to be hers.

4

Poop!

'Where do you think we're going?' Bronte whispered to Tonkins, as they followed their teachers through the grounds.

'Looks like we're heading to the tournament field,' Tonkins said dismally. 'I forgot jousting lessons began this year.'

Jousting!

Bronte imagined herself mounting a mighty

battle boar, its
shaggy coat
escaping from
beneath the plates
of armour, and pulling
her helmet's visor down as
she turned to face her opponent. Her boar pawed
the ground with his trotter, steam snorting from
his snout, before charging forward into the dust.
Bronte raised her lance, holding it steady, ready
to strike –

'Oi, Snotkins.' A voice interrupted her
thoughts. 'Finally made a friend?'

Bronte turned around to see a boy with
cropped hair and a pointy nose. He would have
looked quite nice if it wasn't for the unpleasant
expression on his face. He was flanked by two
boys, who wore sneers that matched his.

'Hi, Lance. Hi, Leo. Pole.' Tonkins said, with no enthusiasm at all. 'Good summer?'

'Yeah, it was pretty busy, you know, what with all the growing and stuff. Something you clearly didn't do.' Lance laughed. 'What do you think, lads? Has Snotkins grown?'

'I reckon he's shrunk,' one of the other boys said, which Bronte thought was a bit rich considering he was the same height as Tonkins.

'Still wearing your stupid hat, Snottykins?' the other boy asked.

Lance glared at him. 'It's *Snot*kins. Not Snottykins. Get it right, Pole.'

Bronte wondered whether Pole was really his name, or a nickname, because he was exceptionally tall, thin and, well, pole-like.

Lance gave Tonkins one last mean smile, before turning his attention to Bronte.

'So, new girl. What made you want to come to this dump?'

'Probably the same reason everyone else does,' Bronte said coolly.

'What school did you go to before?'

Bronte took a deep breath – they were going to find out sooner or later. 'The Palace for Obedient and Outstanding Princesses.'

Lance burst out laughing. 'Wait, you went to POOP? Ha! Hear that, everyone? The new girl loves poop!'

Bronte glanced at Tonkins and rolled her eyes. Like she hadn't heard *that* before.

Leo and Pole started chanting, 'Poop! Poop! Poop!' which seemed to amuse Lance for a moment, but then he shoved Leo in the arm – a signal that silenced them.

'What's *that*?' Lance said, pointing to the toy

Bronte still clutched in her hand.

'Nothing,' Bronte said with a shrug.

'Is that supposed to be a knight?' Pole laughed. 'It is!'

'It's Sir Pen Tine,' Bronte snapped. 'So what?'

'From the rhymes?' This time Lance snorted, he was laughing so hard. 'They're for babies! Everyone knows knights are nothing like that.'

Ignoring the annoying boys, Bronte walked a little faster, shoving her toy deep into her pocket. She refused to care what a forest-fungus like Lance said. There was no way she was going to let anyone ruin this moment.

By the time they reached the flat field, divided by a row of poles joined with a length of rope, Bronte could hardly contain her excitement. She had dreamed for so long of riding a battle boar!

'Oh great,' Tonkins mumbled. 'We're going to be given a demonstration.'

Two squires were helping Sir Ripple into his armour, while Lady Fennel began talking.

'As you've probably guessed by now, you're going to have your first taste of jousting,' she said, with a smile. 'But don't worry, we're not throwing a tournament just yet. We'll start with some simple exercises.'

Sir Ripple strode forward, his armour squeaking with every step. 'Lampton, if you please,' he bellowed.

Moments later, the man in the battered apron appeared, leading the most incredible battle boar. It clearly belonged to Sir Ripple – it had the same flowing golden hair, which looked at odds with its mighty steel-like tusks.

'Lampton looks after the boars,' Tonkins whispered to Bronte. 'That's Guilda the Third, a champion.'

Once Sir Ripple was astride the mighty beast, he rode her towards the front of the class, where Lady Fennel passed him his lance. 'We're going to show you what you'll be doing today. Nothing hard, just simple target practice. How fortunate you are to see a legend in action. Watch closely,' he boomed.

Grass kicked up from under Guilda's trotters as she sped across the field and, when they reached the target, Sir Ripple struck it perfectly with his lance.

The class applauded half-heartedly, and Bronte realised this wasn't the first time they'd seen Sir Ripple 'demonstrating' for them.

'See?' Sir Ripple said, trotting back over. 'Nothing to it!' One of the squires ran up to him with a ladder so he could climb down. Sir Ripple looked around. 'Where's Lampton gone?'

'To fetch the children's boars,' Lady Fennel said, with forced patience.

'How inconvenient,' Sir Ripple complained. 'What am I supposed to do with Guilda?'

'You could take her back to her pen yourself?' Lady Fennel suggested.

Sir Ripple stared at her blankly.

'Or *I* could,' she sighed, taking the reins of the massive creature. 'I won't be long – don't start without me.'

Bronte wasn't listening. She was watching Lampton leading the line of boars towards them. They were smaller than Guilda, but still big enough for their backs to be above the students' heads. Some were black, some were brown, some were black and brown. Some had long shaggy coats, others had tight curly hair, while some just had short, wiry fur. But they all had long, impressive tusks sprouting from either side of their snout.

The steward assigned each student a boar, and Bronte practically held her breath as she waited for her turn. Then her heart sank. Before her stood the strangest-looking creature. Short, no tusks, pinkish skin with tufts of hair – Bronte's battle boar looked more like a common hog!

The other students noticed and started to giggle.

'The princess has a pigling!' Lance snorted, creasing over with laughter.

'Now, now,' Sir Ripple said, coming over. 'A pigling he may be, but Pig is a valiant steed.'

'Pig?' Bronte asked, looking dubiously from the pigling to her teacher.

Sir Ripple ignored her and, instead of passing her the small mounting block, to Bronte's horror, he began to lift her up in the most undignified manner. 'Tell you what, as you're new, you can try the jousting first!' He plonked her onto Pig's shiny metal saddle and shoved a lance into her hand.

'But Sir Ripple, I've never even ridden one bef—'

Sir Ripple never got to hear what she was

saying, because as he slapped Pig's bottom, the pigling shot forward, leaving Bronte clinging on for dear life. He might be smaller than the other boars, but there was nothing wrong with his speed!

'WHOAaaAAARRGGHH!'

Bronte screamed, the lance quickly dropping from her grip as she fumbled for the reins, while bouncing up and down on the prancing pigling. At POOP, the princesses rode pronklets, dainty creatures who slowly and gracefully leaped through the air. Riding them was nothing like this and Bronte had no idea what she was doing.

Pig stormed straight towards the edge of the field and Bronte panicked as the hedge approached.

'Stop, Pig!' she cried out. 'Stop, *please!*'

And stop he did. Suddenly and unexpectedly, so that his trotters skidded through the dirt and Bronte went flying over his head, over the hedge and belly-flopped, **SPLAT**, face down in the muck heap on the other side.

'Feathers!' she groaned, kneeling up, rubbing her eyes clean of the smelly, sticky mess and spitting straw from her mouth. Still, she was in one piece. And though she was covered in manure from head to foot, it had at least offered a soft landing.

Seconds later, the rest of her class peered over the hedge, Sir Ripple looking disgusted at the sight before him.

'Urggh!' the boys cried out, holding their noses.

'Look!' Lance shouted. 'The pigling took the princess back to POOP! Where she belongs!'

Everyone ran off laughing, apart from Tonkins, who started to scramble over the hedge towards her. Bronte waved him away, cheeks burning with embarrassment as she tried to wipe off the muck and only succeeded in making things worse.

'I don't need any help, I'm fine,' she snapped.

Tonkins's face fell and Bronte instantly felt bad.

'I'll take Pig back to his pen then,' he said. 'If you're sure?'

'I'm *fine*,' she said again, wanting him to go away.

Because she wasn't fine. Not even a little bit. Her first day at knight school had ended in humiliation. The last thing she needed was Tonkins seeing her cry as well.

Disappointing Truths

Bronte woke up the next morning without opening her eyes. She almost couldn't face the day waiting for her. Yesterday had been so mortifying that, after a long bath, she hadn't been hungry for tea, and once she had been shown her treehouse sleeping quarters, she didn't leave.

The dorm room was amazing. Vines trailed

down the walls, bright with songflowers, and there were hammocks for five other students strung up between posts. But she was all alone.

She missed her best friend, Ellie. They'd shared a dorm at POOP since reception class and she always made everything better. In fact, they'd been inseparable since their first-ever day at school, when Bronte had been shy, and had hovered nervously in a corner. Then she'd seen another girl who looked just as anxious as she was. Her braided black hair was pinned up on her head, and her bright yellow dress complemented her dark brown skin. Bronte had gone to say hello and that was it, best friends for life!

Ellie would love it here, Bronte thought. *Especially the treehouses.*

But Eliane Blaze, future queen of the Sun Kingdom, wasn't a pointless princess like Bronte.

She didn't have six brothers in line for the throne ahead of her, or anyone else at all, and so she had to have the right kind of princessy education.

There had been no post waiting for Bronte in her room. She didn't know what that meant. Had her parents not bothered to reply because there was nothing to worry about? Or had the thunder trolls reached the palace and squashed it beneath their giant feet? She had scribbled another hasty letter and hung it on the Pixie Post line strung up on her balcony, but it would be at least a day before she could expect a reply.

The many threads of worry knotted like a ball in her stomach. Maybe today would be better. It couldn't actually be much worse.

After skipping tea last night, Bronte was all kinds of hungry. And so, leaving her Sir Pen Tine doll behind on her pillow, she reluctantly climbed out of the treehouse. She took care not to slip on the wet ladder – it was raining really hard! Not quite as hard as back home, but still enough to soak her. The sky flashed with light, taking her by surprise. She hadn't expected to see lightning here. It seemed strange with no rumble of thunder following it.

Tonkins was already in the dining room and waved at her when she walked in.

'Hi,' she said, sitting opposite him. 'Sorry I was snappy yesterday.'

'It's fine,' he said. 'I would have been too. But don't worry, everyone will have forgotten about what happened by now.'

'Hey! It's Snotkins and Poop-face! Thought something smelled bad,' Lance shouted from his table across the way. Leo and Pole knuckle-bumped him in approval.

Bronte looked at Tonkins, who sighed and said, 'OK, well not *everyone*.'

As Bronte reached for a pancake from the pile in front of her, she noticed the newspaper by Tonkins's plate. Her heart leaped. Maybe that would give her some answers about what was happening with the thunder trolls while she waited to hear from her parents.

'Is that yours?' she asked. 'Can I have a look?' She didn't know what she was hoping for more – news that the trolls had been safely returned to the skies above her kingdom, or no news at all.

Tonkins passed her the *Realms' Round-up* paper and she stared in horror at the headline.

Lightning Steeds Lost! Terrible Trolls Trample the Terrain!

'Oh no!' she cried. So her parents hadn't fixed things then. 'Tonkins, this is bad. The thunder trolls are still loose on the ground. Hang on – wait. It's worse than that! It says here that they're in the Mist Queendom . . . That's impossible. The trolls have never left the Storm Kingdom before!'

Tonkins helped himself to another crumpet and dolloped a large spoonful of sugarleaf jam on top. 'Oh really?' He was utterly unconcerned.

But Bronte was alarmed. 'They'll cause havoc!' she cried, before carrying on reading. 'Oh, they are! They're breaking bridges all over the place!'

This was a disaster! For the trolls to fall from the sky was one thing, but to leave the boundaries of the Storm Kingdom? All the unwritten laws and rules of the kingdoms had gone topsy-turvy and Bronte had the sense that anything could happen now.

She read the article again, searching for reassurance and finding none. The trolls seemed to be making their way south. If they came all the way through the Mist Queendom, they'd reach the Heart of the Kingdoms. And what then? Would they stray a little to the west and find their way down to Sir Sebastian's? They would flatten the school without a second thought!

Or worse, what if the thunder trolls veered to the east? The Realm of Education was closer to the Weather Kingdoms than Sir Sebastian's and that's where POOP was, set on the same grounds as the School for Independent and Courageous Kings (affectionately known as SICK) where three of her brothers still went. If the thunder trolls made it there, they could wipe out all the future rulers of every single kingdom, placing the peace at great risk. Not to mention Ellie and

Bronte's brothers might get hurt!

'We have to stop them!' she cried.

Tonkins paused mid bite. 'What?'

'We need to find the lightning steeds. They're the only ones who can fix this. All the kingdoms should send their knights out to find them. Why is no one suggesting this?!'

Tonkins sighed. 'They won't do anything.'

'Why not?'

'Oh, you know knights. They like a good tournament but don't do much else.'

'Don't be silly,' Bronte said in a rush. 'Knights are honourable and brave. Just think about Sir Pen Tine! Remember that story where he had to find the lost prince of the Poppy Kingdom and he searched through every land until he found the prince locked away by those awful villains? He didn't give up, not once! Because that's what knights do. They keep us safe.'

Tonkins scrunched his nose. 'Yeah, maybe they used to. But no one really wants to be one any more because they don't have much of a purpose these days.'

'Don't be ridiculous, of course they have a purpose. They're heroes, defenders of the realms!'

'Um . . .' Tonkins started awkwardly.

'It literally says so in the school prospectus,' Bronte carried on. 'It says: *discover how to become a hero*.'

For a moment Tonkins looked confused, and then he said, 'Ohhhhhh,' drawing out the sound. 'That's what they call the choir. The Heroes. They're really good actually – they've won some pretty prestigious competitions.'

A *choir*? No, no, this wasn't what Bronte had signed up for . . .

She suddenly realised what Tonkins had said before. 'What do you mean, no one wants to be a knight any more?'

Tonkins shrugged. 'Students keep leaving and not many new people are joining. The Realm of Education offers more opportunities now for people who aren't royal, I suppose. You know, like they opened that blacksmith school for people who don't have parents already in the trade. And that animal care place. Oh, and I think there's one for woodworking. There's loads!'

Bronte stared at him. 'Is that the reason why they finally opened up Sir Sebastian's to all children? *To fill spaces?*'

Tonkins had the good grace to look embarrassed.

That's why she was here? Not because of a prophecy declaring her a champion, but to be an extra bum on a seat?

Disappointment sank through her like a stone through water, until it plopped into her stomach, heavy and uncomfortable. Could Tonkins be right? Were knights really not that heroic any more?

Bronte tried to push that thought away to focus on the priority here – the threat of the thunder trolls. She was about to argue that her parents' knights would at least be out defending the kingdom, but then stopped herself. *Would* they? What had she ever seen them *actually* do? Perform ceremonies, entertain in tournaments – there really wasn't much need for them to do anything else when the kingdoms were so peaceful. She'd sort of always assumed the excitement happened away from the castle, that knights were having adventures across the kingdoms, just like in the tales of Sir Pen Tine. Had that all just been wishful thinking created from reading too many stories?

'Anyway, there's nothing we can do,' Tonkins said, gesturing back to the paper. 'The grown-ups can sort it out. All sounds a bit dangerous anyway.'

'Isn't danger part of a knight's job?'

'Not any more.'

Bronte could hardly believe what she was hearing. 'If knights are so rubbish, why do *you* want to be one?'

Tonkins shrugged. 'I'm here for the ceremonial splendour.' And he did a funny little flourish with his hand, making Bronte giggle despite everything. 'Anyway, before you set off to save the kingdoms, I don't suppose you've seen our timetable yet?'

'It better not be jousting again today. Hey, I've been meaning to ask – I've not seen any firecats around. Do you only get them when you leave school for your apprenticeship, like the battle boars?'

'Oh, no, they fly home for the summer while we're not at school,' he said. 'They just haven't come back yet. But they will.'

Bronte couldn't help but smile to herself. Battle boars might have been a disappointment, but surely firecats wouldn't be. The ones that Bronte had seen in the Storm Kingdom were often curled up at their knights' feet. How lovely it would be to have a constant companion by your side.

'Ooh, I know what you'll enjoy,' Tonkins said, taking a huge bite from his crumpet. 'Sword fighting!'

'Do we get to use real swords?' Bronte asked.

'Blunt ones, unfortunately,' Tonkins replied. 'But we started with wooden ones, so it's progress. And we might get to use some other weapons. Like a spear or, oooh, maybe a mace –'

'Like you could lift one of those, Snotkins,' came a sarcastic voice.

Bronte looked up to see sneering Lance walking over with his minions. Tonkins sighed softly, and she saw how his shoulders sagged at their presence.

'And best you're going to get, Poop-face, is a feather duster,' Lance said.

Bronte glared at them. 'Bet I could make you sneeze so hard with it that your brains fell out your nose. Oh wait. You don't have any.'

Turning a particularly unpleasant shade of purple, Lance scowled and skulked off with his friends.

Bronte felt a pang of guilt for being nasty back, but then she saw Tonkins smile and the guilt disappeared.

'That was so breezy!' Tonkins said, giving Bronte a high five. 'Did I use that right?'

Bronte laughed. 'Yep, you did.'

An older student with a bag full of scrolls came up behind Tonkins. 'Year Four, yes?' he asked, before selecting two rolls of parchment and dropping them onto the table.

'Our timetables!' Tonkins snatched one up and scanned it quickly. 'Right. Well, we don't have Weapons class until tomorrow, but we do have Forest Care, which is always good.'

The timetable was nothing like the one at POOP. Instead of Ballroom Dancing, there was Duelling, in place of Diplomacy lessons was Chivalry class. Rather than Dress Mending was Armour Care. At least the timetabled lesson called Lore of the Land sounded vaguely similar to Know the Kingdoms – history, Bronte guessed. And Calligraphy class couldn't be too different to Highnesses' Handwriting.

They got up from the table and Bronte followed Tonkins as he showed her the way to their classroom.

'How is caring for the forest a knightly thing?' Bronte asked.

Tonkins shrugged. 'Think it's more a Sir Sebastian's thing. The forest behind the school needs lots of maintaining and they basically use us to do it. But you get to cuddle cute animals like nibbits and squibbles, so no one minds. Do you have them in the Storm Kingdom?'

'Nope, I've never seen them before,' Bronte said, her excitement growing at the prospect of the lesson. 'By the way, I've been thinking about the quest Lady Fennel set us. Do you have any ideas? I wondered if she might be from another land altogether, where girls have always been knights. Is there a library we can visit? To find out if anywhere like that exists?'

Tonkins nodded. 'Yep, the thin turret right next to the winding willow is the archive tower. We can go there later if you want.'

Bronte was pleased to have a plan. She could also look for ideas of where the lightning steeds might have gone while she was there.

The rain wasn't quite so heavy now, but they

were still getting pretty soggy, so they started to jog. Then Bronte stopped in her tracks. Up ahead, flying low among the rain clouds, was a huge hot-air balloon, trailing several long nets.

'What's that?' she asked in surprise.

'Oh, that's Lampton. He's cloud-catching, you know, to feed the boars. Rumour has it someone broke into the shed yesterday and today. Both times the lock was broken.'

'Really?' Bronte's mind started racing. Yesterday Lampton had told Sir Calliphus the door had been left open. But if the rumours were right, it might be a bit more serious than that. The mystery was too tantalising to ignore. And, as Sir Pen Tine always said, *a puzzle to be solved is the start of a new adventure!*

Tonkins looked at her closely and groaned. 'Oh no. You have a look in your eye.'

'We should go and see what's going on.'

'What the curly custard for?'

'To see if the rumours are true, of course.'

'*Why?* We're supposed to be in class. We can't go wandering off!'

'Why not? We'll be quick.'

Tonkins waited for Bronte to take a few steps before he reluctantly ran after her.

'First you want to find the lightning steeds, now this. Let me put this out there right now, Bronte Tempestra. I am too young to die. All I want is a quiet life!'

With a roll of her eyes and a cheeky grin, Bronte grabbed Tonkins by the arm and raced him across to the boar pens, where the animals were squealing hungrily.

Tonkins hovered anxiously as Bronte headed to the store shed. 'This isn't our problem,' he fretted. 'You know what *will* be? Getting caught and being put in endless detention mucking out pig poo!'

Bronte ignored him as she inspected the padlock. It had definitely been smashed.

She looked up at Tonkins in confusion. 'Why would anyone want to steal clouds?' But before he could answer, something distant caught her eye. 'Tonkins, look!'

Peeping out from behind the boars' armour shed was a creature half their height, with a small squashed face and a very long nose. He was

muttering something under his breath, and Bronte leaned forward to try and hear.

'Boss says be quick, boss says, boss says.'

He looked about and then made a run for it – followed by several other little figures, their arms full of clouds.

'Gnomes!' Bronte said in surprise.

'Yeah, they live in the forest,' Tonkins said. 'They're probably going back there.'

'But what in the green gravy would gnomes want with clouds?'

'Who cares? Everyone knows gnomes like to pinch stuff,' Tonkins replied. 'What I want to know is what the blue bananas happened to their *pants*?!'

A Lesson in Lore

Naturally, Bronte and Tonkins were late to class.

But worse still, it wasn't Lady Fennel waiting for them, but Sir Calliphus.

'And where have you two been?' he demanded.

'Sir, there are gnomes at the boar pens,' Bronte said. 'They're stealing clouds!'

'And what, pray, were you doing at the boar pens, when you were supposed to be here?'

'But, sir, the clouds!'

'Enough! Sit down and stop dripping all over the floor. Honestly, this infernal weather.'

Bronte was furious, but she had no choice other than to follow Tonkins to the bench at the back of the room, hoping not to draw more attention to herself. Sadly her wet shoes had other ideas, squeaking loudly on the polished floor, causing Bronte to wince with every step.

Once she was sitting at her desk and everyone had finally stopped staring, Bronte looked around the classroom. This was the first tower she had entered since arriving and it was far more like home. The traditional regal stone walls and floor were draped in purple velvet furnishings which brought about a pang of homesickness.

But that only made her think of the thunder trolls and stirred the anxiety simmering in her tummy. With those trolls on the loose, they were in danger and seemingly no one was willing to protect them.

'As I was saying before,' Sir Calliphus said, 'due to an error in the timetable, this term your Forest Care classes will be replaced by an extra Lore of the Land lesson.'

Tonkins groaned, then instantly covered his mouth, embarrassed.

'Pole, hand out these textbooks,' Sir Calliphus said, frowning at Tonkins.

On the walls were posters of forest animals and plants – some simple diagrams, others labelled with interesting facts, all of which made Bronte sad that her Forest Care lesson was cancelled. There were cute nibbits, with their floppy pink ears, the squibbles had bushy green tails and the black and white badleys looked super cuddly.

Fixels, according to the poster closest to Bronte, were the rarest forest animals and liked to hide beneath leaves, but their needle-sharp teeth could give a nasty bite. She wanted to meet all of them!

'Bronte Tempestra! Are you paying attention?'

Bronte started, her cheeks flushing red.

'Good, then you can tell me all about the history of the Heart of the Kingdoms, can't you?'

'Um, yes?'

When she said nothing more, Sir Calliphus grew frustrated. 'Then do!'

'Oh, um, well, I know that it is the land in the middle of all the kingdoms, under the rule of no one king or queen, which is why the Realm of Education is set here, because it's neutral.'

Clearly Sir Calliphus hadn't expected her to know even that and he looked irritated. 'Indeed. But can anyone tell me what was here before it became the Heart of the Kingdoms?'

A few hands shot up.

'Yes, Varney?'

'The old Tree Kingdoms.'

Sir Calliphus nodded. 'And of course, it was decided that this school should be built *outside* of the Realm of Education, and instead on the site of the ancient trees that represented the four kingdoms to symbolise our victory. Can anyone name those four kingdoms? Tonkins?'

'Er, Oak, Willow, Maple, Cherry?'

'Precisely. For centuries, these Tree Kingdoms were very important because everyone needed to pass through them if they wished to travel and trade. So what went wrong?'

This time, no one answered.

'They became greedy,' Sir Calliphus said. 'They wanted more money from those travelling their roads, declared themselves the most important kingdoms, and stopped any who disagreed from crossing their borders. Of course, war broke out, and the resulting battles are famous in knight lore. Now open your textbooks and read section one. When you're finished, write me an essay about why the griffin lords and their battalions were banished after the war.'

Varney's hand shot up. 'Because they refused to choose a side, sir. And such disloyalty was not to be tolerated.'

Sir Calliphus sighed wearily. 'I said write me an essay, Varney, not tell the class the answer. Right, any questions?'

This time it was Bronte who put her hand up.

'Yes, Tempestra?'

'Sir Calliphus, the thunder trolls are roaming wild across the kingdoms. Shouldn't we be trying to stop them?'

He glared at her. 'I meant questions regarding your work.'

'But, sir, what if they reach the Realm of Education?' Just as no one seemed bothered about the whereabouts of the lightning steeds, there was shockingly little concern for the schools full of the kingdoms' future monarchs. Not to mention the other schools in the realm. 'They could attack the princes and princesses, and isn't it our duty as knights to protect them?'

The whole class had fallen silent now, waiting to see what Sir Calliphus would say.

He was quiet a long time before he spoke. 'Three things, Tempestra. First, it is not up to the knights to fix the problems of *your* kingdom. Second, the students at both the Palace for Obedient and Outstanding Princesses, and the School for Independent and Courageous Kings, are guarded by the grim gargoyles, which, as you know perfectly well, are roaming stone statues that not even the thunder trolls would dare cross. And third – and this is the most important of all – READ SECTION ONE OF YOUR TEXTBOOK!'

Bronte stared at the table, quietly seething. Of course she knew the grim gargoyles guarded the schools, but everyone had said the thunder trolls would never leave the Storm Kingdom, and look what had happened! Surely nothing could be taken for granted any more.

This was so frustrating! She had been a pointless princess all her life, and she had made her peace with that. But to finally make it to Sir Sebastian's and discover that all she had to look forward to was becoming a pointless knight too?

No.

No one wanted to stop the thunder trolls? No

one cared about POOP and SICK? Then fine. She'd have to save them herself.

While also figuring out what those pesky bare-bottomed gnomes were up to.

And catching up with all the work she was hopelessly behind on.

Nevertheless! She alone would save the kingdoms, setting off on her noble quests astride a loyal battle boar, putting right all the wrongs of the –

She caught Sir Calliphus glaring murderously at her, and started to read.

The Gauntlet Run

After only two days, Bronte was struggling. With so many different lessons to the ones at POOP, she was starting from scratch in every subject. She *still* hadn't heard from her parents, and there had been no more news about the trolls in the morning paper. She took a deep breath. At least today was her first Weapons class and she was looking forward to taking out her frustrations on a straw dummy with a blunt sword.

As she and Tonkins dashed through the rain towards the large building where the Weapons class took place, a fork of lightning darted from the sky, striking the ground near the forest.

'Blue bananas!' Tonkins exclaimed. 'I don't know how you live in a kingdom where this is normal. Usually we only get a bit of drizzle.'

This was definitely Storm Kingdom weather. At home, Bronte loved it. She loved how at night the sky was heavy with black clouds, like giant rocks floating through the air. How the ground below shook and echoed as the thunder trolls' massive feet struck the clouds, crashing and banging as they ran across them. How moments later the sky flashed bright as the lightning steeds stampeded in pursuit of the thunder trolls. Sparks would fly from the horses' hooves, striking the world below as dazzling bolts. At home, that was magical.

But here, the constant rain and promise of a storm seemed all wrong.

Was it because the thunder trolls were on the loose – a sign they were heading this way and likely to trample the school to the ground with those massive feet of theirs? Why was no one doing anything to stop them? And despite Sir Calliphus insisting the grim gargoyles were the perfect defence, she wasn't convinced the young royals were safe from danger either. Frustration made her head ache.

'Is this weather your fault, storm girl?' Lance hissed, as they took cover in the classroom.

Bronte ignored him.

'Are you a weather witch?' Lance continued.

Tonkins looked anxiously from Lance to

Bronte and back again, sensing a trap.

'Don't be stupid,' Bronte replied, causing Tonkins to relax slightly. 'Weather witches are really rare,' she added, causing Tonkins to groan.

'They're made up,' Lance sneered. 'Like your stupid Sir Pen Tine. Seriously, how old are you?'

His nasty teasing was interrupted by Lady Fennel clapping her hands to command attention.

'We'll begin our lesson in a moment but, while we wait, I just wondered if anyone has solved the task I set for you. Do any of you know how I came to be knight?'

Varney quickly raised his hand. 'You went to summer school?'

Lady Fennel smiled at him. 'Good try, but no. Anyone else?'

Bronte was relieved when no one else offered

an answer. She wanted to win that prize but so far, all she and Tonkins had learned in the archives was that Sir Sebastian's was the only known school for squires in the recorded lands. Which put an end to their theory. She'd also found nothing to suggest the lightning steeds would go anywhere else but the Storm Kingdom, so it had been an entirely frustrating visit and Tonkins had been most put out that they'd missed dessert for it.

Just then Sir Ripple came striding in. Were there no other teachers at this school?

'You're late,' Lady Fennel said to him, but he brushed her away with a wave of his hand.

'Good day to you, young squires! You'll be delighted to hear I have yet another wonderful challenge for you today. As you undoubtedly know, *Knights Weekly* named me number one in their "Giants of the Gauntlet" feature. They marvelled at the grace of Sir Double R, and today I am willing to share my tips and tricks with you. Well, some of them at least – don't want to give everything away! But together we'll learn a bend here, a leap there, cheating even death itself –'

'If Sir Double R doesn't stop talking, there won't be time for everyone to have a turn,' Lady Fennel said drily.

Sir Ripple looked mildly put out but recovered quickly. 'May I present to you, my gauntlet run!' And he pulled a cord on the curtain behind him, revealing an alarming obstacle course on a wooden platform. With a gleeful grin, he pushed a big lever that turned a set of cogs and the obstacles started to move, fast and furiously.

Bronte's eyes widened in horror. *Oh great*, she thought to herself. *Today's the day I die.*

At that moment, Sir Calliphus appeared at the door. 'Lady Fennel, a word?'

'Of course,' she said, before looking sternly at Sir Ripple. 'Don't start without me, understood?'

She left without waiting for a reply, but clearly Sir Ripple wasn't listening.

'Right, everyone, watch carefully,' he said. He climbed the steps and cracked his knuckles. 'I shall show you how to stay alive!'

With a narrowing of his eyes, he sprinted towards the first obstacle, a swinging mace. Timing it perfectly, he dashed past without getting thwacked aside. He struck a dramatic pose before rolling underneath a clump of hanging spear heads, their points gleaming cruelly. Next up, a row of three axe-heads swinging haphazardly. Sir Ripple spun and twisted through the gaps with ease, like a ballet dancer. Then he leaped onto the hanging rope above a carpet of blades and swung until he had enough momentum to land cat-like beyond them. Pausing only to flash the students a wide grin, he ran past the final obstacle of twin war hammers, which were bashing inwards so that, if he wasn't fast enough, he'd be squished flat. But once again Sir Ripple made it through unharmed, leaping off the stage and taking a bow to the students' begrudging applause.

'Nothing to it!' he declared, as if he hadn't just done the scariest thing Bronte had ever seen. 'Right, who wants to go first?'

He was kidding, right?

'Nobody?' Sir Ripple sounded disappointed.

'Ladies first,' Lance said, giving Bronte an evil smile.

Bronte flashed Lance a vicious look.

'Ahh, yes. Tempestra, come on up!'

Bronte looked frantically at Tonkins, who seemed as panicked as she was.

'Um, sir, didn't Lady Fennel say we should wait?' Tonkins tried desperately to help his friend.

'Tish, tosh!' Sir Ripple boomed. 'Fear not, Tempestra, you know what to do,' he said.

'Excuse me?' Bronte said, confused.

'Well, you saw me do it. Copy what I did!'

That was it? He wanted her to face this lethal death run with no more instruction than that?!

'Sir, I really think –' But Bronte was interrupted by Sir Ripple's determined shove.

'Timing is everything . . . Now, GO!' he shouted.

The world disappeared around Bronte. There was nothing but the terrifying ball of death hurtling back and forth in front of her. She had to pull herself together.

Feet firm, head high. Be brave.

YEAH RIGHT!

She counted slowly and carefully, judging how long she had to sneak past it.

One . . . two . . . three . . . run!

Time slowed as the **SWOOOOOOSH** of the mace echoed back towards her. And then somehow she was on the other side of it, genuinely stunned to find herself still intact and still breathing.

Beyond her pounding heartbeat she could hear the other students, cheering her on. '*Bronte! Bronte! BRONTE!*'

Next she dropped to the floor of the platform, and tried to roll underneath the spears like Sir Ripple had done. But it was harder than it looked and she soon found herself stuck beneath the deadly points.

Oh, come on!

She tried to wriggle but shifted her weight too far upwards and gasped as she stared directly at a shiny blade just a fraction away from her eye.

Eeek!

She lay there, frozen, not knowing what to do. Why would she? She shouldn't be here!

In the distance, she heard someone laugh. Lance. And then, sheer stubbornness kicked in, outweighing her fear.

Carefully she used her hands to slowly push her body along and eventually she slithered out from beneath the spears like a snake, only to find herself confronted with the swinging battle-axes. How in the green gravy was she supposed to get past *those*?

She tried counting, like she had with the mace, but she couldn't find the right rhythm.

Feathers! Should she close her eyes and hope for the best? Probably not.

Here goes!

She made to step forward, but at that moment every person in the room started screaming and Bronte, with her foot paused mid-air, was suddenly aware of a whole new threat.

A flock of flying creatures had burst through the door! They were big and very angry. To Bronte's horror, their vast thin wings seemed to be edged with jagged sharp metal. The class had dropped to the floor in a desperate attempt to avoid being cut to ribbons. Bronte didn't remember seeing anything like this on the posters in the Forest Care classroom! As most of the creatures flapped around the room, several headed towards her, their bodies black and yellow, their curved wings bright and multi-coloured. She was trapped, stuck between sharp spears and chaotic axes. But then she realised the obstacle course offered her some protection. Bronte could only crouch low and hope she didn't get hurt.

As the intruders beat their strange metal-tipped wings against the swinging battle-axes, a fine powder fell from them. No sooner had it touched Bronte's skin than the burning and itching began.

'**OW!**' Bronte cried, rubbing frantically at her arms, then her neck, until she didn't have enough hands to reach all the hurting parts.

The other children were rolling on the floor, suffering from the same poisonous powder that fell like dandruff from the monsters.

The room was filled with an entire swarm, and

Bronte wondered for the second time that day if this was the moment she would die.

'Hey!' a loud voice shouted. 'Leave now, or face my blades!'

Bronte looked up to see Lady Fennel, her two swords raised high as she prepared to battle the creatures.

Not once did she flinch as the flying intruders launched themselves at her. The knight's blades met the metal wings of death and blocked their attack. On and on she fiercely fought, protecting her class, until the creatures screeched and wailed into retreat, leaving behind a class of trembling and distressed children.

Firecats

Lady Fennel hurried to the gauntlet run and pulled the lever, switching it off. Once the weapons had stopped moving, Lady Fennel went to Bronte and stretched out her hand.

'Down you come, Tempestra.'

Bronte clutched Lady Fennel's gloved fingers and leaped safely to the ground. She managed a wobbly smile.

'Thanks. What *were* those things?'

Lady Fennel frowned. 'They looked a bit like forrerflies.'

'More like *horrorflies*!' Tonkins said, joining them, his skin blotchy and red. 'Forrerflies are normally tiny and I don't remember them *ever* having bladed wings! Or giving me an itchy rash!'

'No,' Lady Fennel said, her frown deepening. She looked around the classroom at the other children whimpering.

'I want to go home,' Varney cried, as a boy called Higgles comforted him.

Pole had gone a strange grey colour in shock, and Leo was scratching himself and muttering, 'What the curly custard just happened?'

Lance, meanwhile, was shaking the itching powder from his head. 'Look at the state of my hair!'

Lady Fennel clapped her hands, demanding their attention. 'Everyone! Outside into the rain. Let the water soothe your skin.'

At that moment Sir Ripple emerged from his hiding place behind the curtain.

'What were you thinking?' Lady Fennel exploded at him. Sir Ripple wilted beneath her fury.

'They were nothing to do with me. I have no idea where those creatures came from, honest!'

Lady Fennel narrowed her eyes. 'I wasn't talking about the creatures. I want to know why on *earth* would you let a student run your training gauntlet?'

'Oh!' Sir Ripple became flustered. 'But that was the point of the lesson!'

'No, the point of the lesson was to show them what a real gauntlet run was like and *then* show them the practice one I had set up.' And she strode angrily over to another curtain and pulled it open.

Behind it was a similar obstacle course to the one Bronte had just attempted, only instead of deadly weapons, the obstacles were made of sacks stuffed with straw.

'Ohhhhh,' Sir Ripple said, drawing the sound out.

'Oh, indeed. Perhaps cowering behind a curtain is the best place for you.'

He made some blustering noises, before sweeping out of the room.

Lady Fennel sighed. 'Come on,' she said to Bronte and Tonkins. 'Let's join the others.'

The moment the rain hit Bronte's skin, the

nasty powder was washed away and the horrid itching stopped.

With the students finally soothed, Lady Fennel called for everyone to be quiet. 'Well, that was a bit of unexpected excitement, wasn't it? But we have far more wonderful things to think about. Sir Calliphus was just telling me that the firecats have returned.'

There was an enthusiastic murmuring among the students, but Bronte wasn't quite so ready to forget.

'Is that *it*?' Bronte whispered to Tonkins as they followed their classmates.

'What do you mean?'

'Tonkins, we just got attacked by killer *horror*flies! And now we're acting like nothing happened?'

'Well, what do you want them to do, Bronts?

They've gone, so what's the problem?'

'We're knights! Shouldn't we be doing knight-like things?'

'Lady Fennel chased them all away. That was pretty breezy!'

'Yes, but where've they gone? Why were they so big? And why the green gravy did they have metal blades on their wings?'

Tonkins shrugged. 'You want to chase danger *far* too much, Bronts. Come on, we're going to see the firecats! Aren't you excited?'

No, she wasn't, Bronte thought furiously. She was stressed. Sir Ripple had nearly got her killed on a gauntlet run. She'd been attacked by *horror*flies. And everyone was acting like the world was *normal*. It was turning into another far-from-perfect day. It reminded her of when Sir Pen Tine had gone on a quest to catch the slubber-slobber hiding beneath the sand in the desert between the Floral Kingdoms and the Forgotten Kingdoms. No one else had cared because it hadn't been affecting them. But he hadn't let other people bring him down. Bronte told herself that she must try to do the same.

As they trailed across the grounds and down the hillside, they passed the forest to their left. Bronte stared at it, bewitched. It was dark beyond the first few trees, the strong wind whipping at the branches, threatening to shake the forest's secrets free. It was one of the last remnants of the old kingdoms and Bronte longed to explore it. Oh, if only the Forest Care lessons hadn't been cancelled! She might have actually done well in that class.

Several bolts of lightning suddenly shot down into the heart of the forest.

No one else seemed to have noticed, too busy paying attention to the steep steps they were walking down, but Bronte was unsettled. Nothing felt right.

'Bronts, we're here,' Tonkins said.

At the bottom of the hill was a cliff face, with many cave openings in its surface. But there was no sign of any firecats.

'Where are they?' Bronte whispered to Tonkins.

He shrugged.

'Where do they migrate to over the summer?'

'No one really knows. I always worry that Dotty won't come back though, that she'll have forgotten me.'

'Why would she?' Bronte said. 'After all, the firecats choose their knight, right? Not the other way round.'

'True,' he said, sounding reassured.

'Why do they come to the caves?' Bronte asked, her nerves making her talkative. 'Rather than flying straight to their knights?'

'It's tradition,' Tonkins replied with a hint of awe, before considering and adding, 'Plus they like eating the foogle-fungal that grows in the caves.'

'Everyone, quiet!' Lady Fennel called. 'Let's give our firecats time to recognise who's out here.'

She stepped closer to Bronte and whispered gently, 'Are you ready? I promise you'll love this.'

Bronte nodded, trying to ignore the butterflies in her tummy. The class stood in silence and waited, the kind of magical silence where you know something amazing is about to happen.

And then it did.

Fire blasted out of the cave openings, followed moments later by a dozen colourful, winged cats. Bronte gasped as she watched them soar through the air, sweeping and swooping, painting the sky with fire and creating a rainbow of their own smoke. It was a sight to behold and all Bronte's doubts and worries fell away. She wouldn't have missed this sight for all the world.

They twisted and turned, performing their airborne dance to perfection, before slowly beginning to dive towards the children.

'Dotty!' Tonkins cried out as his firecat flew into his arms, throwing him to the ground and pinning him there while she enthusiastically licked his face.

Bronte had suspected Dotty might be spotty, but in fact she was black with white stripes, one of her wings was black, the other white. She had small curled horns, and Bronte thought she was absolutely beautiful.

She looked around at the other reunited knights and firecats. Each one really was different. One was yellow with green stripes and two wings on each side, another was pink with blue stripes and wonky wings. Some had little horns, some didn't. But they were all a similar size, reaching to about their knight's knees. And they all had stripes of one kind or another.

Still, no firecat appeared for her.

Anxiously Bronte glanced over to see whether Lady Fennel might help. But she was busy nuzzling her own firecat. It was bigger than the students' firecats, reaching just above Lady Fennel's waist, and looked jet black, its stripes so similar in colour you could hardly tell them apart. It had golden eyes and six magnificent golden wings, as well as one single golden paw.

'How big do they grow?' Bronte asked Tonkins, as he untangled himself from Dotty's affectionate attack.

'Apparently they never stop growing. Some ancient ones must be massive, but they don't come back to these lands once their knights die. The largest one we know of was bonded with a knight who lived to be a hundred and four, and that towered over him!'

Bronte thought about how sad it must be for

the firecats once their knight's died. Did they mourn them back in their homelands for as long as they lived? And how long was that? Was there a place full of lonely firecats remembering their old friends?

'Class, once you're reunited with your firecat, can you please make your way back up to the school grounds? There are other students waiting to come down,' Lady Fennel instructed.

Slowly the squires began to climb home, and Tonkins looked uncertainly at Bronte.

'Want me to stay?' he asked.

She shook her head. 'No, it's fine.' Honestly, if no firecat was coming to choose her, she'd rather he wasn't around to see it.

'OK, I'll save you a seat at tea. Good luck!'

Bronte watched as he walked away, Dotty running loyally at his heels. Smoke curled through the air so that all the world smelled of bonfires.

Lady Fennel came over to join her. The knight's firecat seemed even bigger close up, his golden eyes glinting with fierce intelligence, his teeth bared ever so slightly. Bronte took a step back.

'Shadow won't hurt you,' Lady Fennel said. 'And don't worry, sometimes it can take a while, but they always come.'

'What if I'm not meant to be a knight?' Bronte said quietly. 'I've got everything wrong so far.'

'Never underestimate firecats,' Lady Fennel said. 'They don't care what you look like, only what's in your heart. Not even a disguise could stop a firecat from finding its true knight.'

Before Bronte could reply, there was a flicker of movement from the cave closest to them.

A tiny ball of fluff rolled out. Little stripes of white shimmered down his back like silver against his pale blue fur. As he tumbled, he got tangled up in his long tail and bumped over the row of three stubby horns between his ears. He tried to flap his tiny wings, but didn't manage to lift far from the ground. Instead, he bounced towards Bronte where he collapsed, exhausted. He puffed a little, but no flames came out. Bronte reached down, scooped him into her arms and beamed at Lady Fennel.

'Well, well,' said Lady Fennel. 'A firekitten.'

'A fire*kitten*?' Bronte exclaimed. 'Is that why he can't breathe fire yet?'

Lady Fennel frowned. 'No, they usually do that from birth.'

'Maybe he's a slow learner, like me,' Bronte said. 'We can be misfits together!'

'You're doing fine, Tempestra,' Lady Fennel assured her, but she continued to look at the firekitten with interest. 'How curious,' she murmured. 'I've only ever seen one firekitten before.'

'You have?' And then suddenly the quest Lady Fennel had given them made perfect sense. 'Oh, wait! You were here, weren't you? All along! You disguised yourself as a boy, didn't you? That's how you trained to be a knight! And you met Shadow here too? And he was a firekitten!'

'Full marks, Bronte Tempestra,' Lady Fennel said, looking proud. 'I knew you would be the one to solve my mystery. It wouldn't even occur to most of the boys that anything they wanted to do would be forbidden to them. So yes, I'm afraid I was naughty, and came here in disguise.'

'But did anyone ever find out? Did you get into trouble?'

'Oh yes, they found out. On the very last day before I left for my apprenticeship. I waited until the leavers' assembly to reveal the truth: that they'd all got their butts kicked by a girl.'

'Breezy!' Bronte sighed, her admiration for Lady Fennel quadrupling.

Lady Fennel chuckled. 'They weren't impressed. Went to a lot of effort to make sure no one else found out. My apprenticeship disappeared, which was a bad thing for me. You see, I didn't come from a noble family, I was a miller's daughter. My deceit brought shame on my family, and I wasn't welcome back home in the Ruby Kingdom. I've been making a living as a travelling performer for years. Until Sir Calliphus wrote and offered me a job.'

'Didn't that bother you?' Bronte asked. 'After they treated you so badly?'

Lady Fennel nodded. 'But I didn't come back for him. I came for all the children like me, who dreamed of being a knight but hadn't been allowed before. For people like you.'

Bronte blushed shyly, even as her heart swelled with gratitude.

As if sensing she'd made Bronte self-conscious, Lady Fennel stroked the firekitten's chin. 'So, what are you going to call this little chap?'

'Blue,' Bronte said, thrilled that his colour matched the streak in her own hair.

'Perfect,' Lady Fennel said. 'Come on, we

should get back to school.'

The two of them began their journey up the hill – Bronte chuckling as Blue buzzed around Shadow, much to the older firecat's dismay.

'Hey!' Bronte said, suddenly. 'Does this mean I actually won something?'

Lady Fennel laughed. 'It does indeed. You have won the most precious gift of all, self-belief.' She stopped walking, squatted down so she was the same height as Bronte, and looked at her intensely. 'Let me tell you something. A knight's greatest weapon isn't a sword, or a lance. It's this.' And she pressed her fingers to her head. 'If you take time to use your brain, then there is no quest you cannot overcome. Some might think gracing the cover of *Knights Weekly* or being a jousting champion is the measure of a knight, but that's all show. Heart and head, Bronte. That's the true

worth of a knight. And you have plenty of both.'
She stood up and smoothed down her trousers.
'And now, you are the first in the class to have
completed a quest. What, I wonder, will be your
next?'

Hopefully one with an actual prize! Bronte
thought to herself. Self-belief was all very nice,
but she'd have preferred a shiny sword!

Into the Forest

Bronte headed towards the dining hall for tea with a newfound confidence and Blue wrapped round her neck like a scarf, only to see Tonkins running towards her, waving his hat, with Dotty at his feet.

'Emergency assembly!' he shouted. 'Hurry!'

She followed Tonkins into the assembly hall to join the gathered students.

Sir Calliphus was standing on the stage, with a firecat that could only be his, with its similar bushy facial hair. Beside him was an ancient bearded man, who was sitting in a chair with his eyes shut. A large white and grey firecat was curled round his feet, snoring.

'Is that the headmaster?' Bronte whispered to Tonkins, who nodded, while Blue and Dotty booped noses in greeting.

Sir Calliphus cleared his throat for silence. 'Sir Blake wishes to inform you of some important developments.'

'Can't he speak for himself?' Bronte asked, but Tonkins shushed her.

'As you know,' Sir Calliphus continued, 'today the school came under attack by abnormally large forrerflies.'

At last! Bronte thought. *The knights are*

finally going to do something!

'Sir Blake would like to assure you all that there is absolutely *nothing* to worry about, and that we have no concerns regarding your safety. There has been no sign of the forrerflies since, and so we see no reason to take any further action.'

What?! Bronte couldn't believe it.

'However,' Sir Calliphus said, 'to be on the safe side, Sir Blake has decided that for now, the forest is to be entirely out of bounds to all students.'

A cry of objection echoed round the hall, while the firecats puffed smoke in protest. Well, except for Blue, who tried, but still nothing came out apart from a small snort. Sir Calliphus raised his hands, demanding silence.

'I know this will come as a disappointment, but all access is now forbidden, and all Forest

Care classes cancelled. Thank you. Now, please make your way to the dining hall, where your tea awaits.'

Bronte and Tonkins looked at each other, as the students began to file out.

'That's *it*?' Bronte whispered to Tonkins. 'I mean, our Forest Care lessons were already cancelled, so what difference does this make? Don't they want to know what those *horror*flies were? Where they came from? Anything?'

'At least they've closed the forest.'

'How does that help? We were attacked *outside* of the forest. It doesn't make any sense!'

'No,' Tonkins said absently. 'I wonder what's for tea?'

This was ridiculous. As Tonkins listed the *many* foods he hoped to eat, Bronte quietly seethed. How could the knights be this *useless*?

There were thunder trolls rampaging, poisonous *horror*flies swarming, naked gnomes thieving–
and no one was doing anything about any of them!

As Dotty cowered from the rain, and Blue stuck out his tongue to catch raindrops, Bronte looked to the heavens in frustration but noticed something strange in the distance. She squinted to see better.

'Tonkins,' she said, nudging his arm. 'Look!'

'What?' he moaned, as she pulled him away from everyone else.

'Over there, above the trees! What is that?'

'Looks like a floating net.' Tonkins still wasn't interested.

'No, there's something else, something caught in it! I think it might be alive!' she cried. And as if the net had heard her, it suddenly dropped, disappearing into the trees below. 'It's gone! Into the old forest!'

'Good, can I have my tea now?'

'Will you *stop* thinking about your stomach! We have to investigate.'

Tonkins glared at her. 'I'm sorry, it sounded like you just told me you wanted to break like a thousand school rules in one go.'

'Oh, come on! Where's your sense of adventure?'

'I don't have one! I have a very strong sense of self-preservation!'

'But whatever it is might need help. Don't you want to be a proper knight?'

'You mean face danger for the greater good?'

Bronte nodded.

'Not interested,' Tonkins said, lifting Dotty up.

Bronte tried again. 'Come on, you don't want

me to go alone, do you?'

Eventually he sighed, dramatic as ever. '*Fine!* But let's hurry, I'm going to be so cross if all the cake is gone by the time we get back.'

They sneaked away towards the forest, which loomed dark in the dimming sky and dismal weather. Blue tried to hide behind Bronte's hair, and Dotty quivered in Tonkins's arms. Bronte didn't blame them – she wasn't feeling so brave any more either!

She took a deep breath. 'Right, Tonks, you can be my forest guide, point out the cute animals and make sure I don't do anything stupid like pick a poisonous berry or something. And hopefully we'll get a clue as to just *what* is going on.'

Tonkins grunted as he fell into step beside her, putting Dotty down onto the ground. Blue sprang from Bronte's shoulder to ride on Dotty's back.

The forest was full of shadows, cast by the remaining light filtering through the leaves, and the howling wind whipped the rain into their faces, unnerving Bronte.

How much history had these trees seen? Did they remember when they were part of a powerful kingdom? Had they minded generations of hopeful young squires playing among them?

One thing was certain – this forest was awake and watching, and goosebumps prickled up Bronte's arms.

'Here, deep in the undergrowth of the forest, a perfect specimen lies,' Tonkins said, putting on a silly voice. 'Soft, green, some might call it nature's mattress.'

Bronte looked to see what he was pointing at. 'You mean moss?'

Tonkins glared at her. 'I'm doing that guy

who travels round tournaments, teaching people about nature.' He continued in the silly voice. 'It lies in perfect harmony with its neighbour, the messy but ever-present substance that carpets the forest floor.'

'What, mud?'

'Look,' Tonkins said, in his own voice. 'It isn't easy to do this when, frankly, I'm pretty distracted by the fact that the forest is *so creepy*!'

'Shhh!' Bronte pressed her finger to her lips. 'We don't want to ... *attract* anything.'

They walked quietly on, searching for any sign of the net that had fallen, and listening for any sound of something in distress.

But after a while, as they ventured deeper into the forest, Bronte frowned. 'Is it weird that we haven't actually *seen* a single animal yet?'

Tonkins looked around and nodded.

Fear crept up her neck like a rash. 'You don't think something's *eating* them?'

'Well, I do now!' He shuffled anxiously. 'I think we should go back, Bronts. Maybe whatever was in that net was caught for good reason.'

Ignoring him, Bronte continued pushing past tree branches and following the narrow path. Blue leaped from Dotty's back and onto the ground, pawing at the leaves.

'What is it, Blue?' Bronte asked, going to see what the firekitten had found. When she saw it, she moved Blue quickly away. 'Careful, it's a knife!'

Tonkins came over and frowned. 'Someone must have lost it,' he said.

'It's not that sharp,' Bronte said. 'We should take it back to school though. We don't want an animal to hurt themselves on it.' Bronte tucked the knife carefully into her belt.

'At this rate, we might need it to defend ourselves,' Tonkins said, looking anxiously around.

They walked a little while longer, with still no sign of anything having fallen into the forest. But then a low growl echoed through the trees.

Bronte and Tonkins stopped dead.

'Please tell me that's the normal sound one of those cute woodland animals makes,' Bronte whispered.

'You have *no* idea how much I want to tell you that.'

'I think it's coming from over here,' Bronte said, tiptoeing cautiously towards the noise.

'What are you *doing*?' Tonkins hissed.

Blue seemed to agree, tugging at her tunic, urging her to turn back.

'This is what we came to find out, Tonks.'

'Are you *kidding*?'

Bronte fixed him with a stern expression
and then, using the trees for cover, edged slowly
forward, as the growl grew louder. Despite what
she'd said to Tonkins, her heart was hammering
incredibly fast.

Peering around the wide trunk of an old tree,
Bronte's eyes widened.

The animal was black and white, the size of a
small horse, with its muzzle snuffling through the
undergrowth, grumbling and growling as it went.

Bronte's whole body relaxed and she turned
back to call to Tonkins. 'It's all right, it's only a
badley!' She recognised it from the posters in the
classroom, though admittedly it wasn't quite as
cuddly as the picture had suggested.

Tonkins came up behind her and grabbed her

arm. 'Um, Bronts, that's no badley.'

'Yes, it is, it looks just like one.'

'Yeah, apart from the fact that a normal badley is smaller than Dotty!'

No sooner had he said that, than the creature – which most definitely was *not* any ordinary badley – sniffed the bark of a nearby tree, opened its jaw so wide that it stretched down to the ground and then sank its teeth into the tree trunk, tearing out a massive chunk as easily as if it were made of cake.

'Back away,' Bronte barely whispered. '*Slowly.*'

But when she glanced behind, she saw

Tonkins had already legged it! Bronte didn't want to wait to see how the badley might react and so she ran for it too, slowing down only when they were sure they'd put enough distance between them and the mutant creature.

'Something terrible is happening here!' Bronte exclaimed.

'You *think*? First the *horror*flies, now a *bad*ley, what nightmare's next?'

'Oh, you humans are all the same,' an unfamiliar voice said.

'**AAARRRGGGGGGHHH!!!**' Bronte and Tonkins clung to each other for dear life, whirling around to see where the voice was coming from.

'Moan, moan, moan, that's all you do. Thundering hooves, you're not the only ones having a trying day!'

Lord Errol

With the body of a lion and the head of an eagle, Bronte and Tonkins found themselves standing in front of a real live griffin. Bronte could hardly believe it – hadn't they been banished for centuries?

Yet here he was, lying on the forest floor, tangled and trapped in a cloud net!

Bronte hurried towards him. 'Never fear,

Mr Griffin! We're here to rescue you!' she cried, victoriously.

'Mr? *Mr*?' The griffin was horrified. 'Do you know who you're speaking to, small human? I am Lord Errol of the First Battalion of Griffins. Oh, the mortification!' He closed his eyes and shook his head. 'To be reduced to this, needing help from simple humans. I shall never live it down. The sheer embarrassment, the horror. The shame! And to be seen in such a state of undress!'

'He goes on a bit, doesn't he?' Tonkins whispered to Bronte, who couldn't help but smile. Tonkins talked more than anyone she'd ever met!

'We saw you fall from the sky,' Bronte said. 'We came to help.'

But Tonkins held her back. 'Are you sure we should? Everyone knows griffins are vicious. It might eat us as soon as it's free.'

'I beg your pardon!' Lord Errol was deeply offended. 'These are scandalous lies that dishonour the griffin name. But by all means, run home, small coward. Leave me to the mercy of those others.'

'What others?' Bronte asked, confused.

'The other, *big* humans,' Lord Errol said. 'They were most delighted to discover me and went off to fetch a wagon. I would prefer not to be here when they return.'

Bronte turned to Tonkins. 'Who else could be here? Teachers?'

Lord Errol rolled his eyes. 'My dear small human, these ruffians were not from the school. From what I could deduce, they were brothers – one called Elon, the other Hollis – and they were searching for something they had lost. If I am any judge of character, they were a villainous pair and up to no good.'

'Trespassers?' Bronte wondered.

'We need to go back and tell the headmaster,' Tonkins said. 'This is serious, Bronts.'

'If you free me,' Lord Errol said, 'I shall take the greatest pleasure in hunting those fiends down and dealing with them myself.'

'We're not going to let you out so you can eat them!' Tonkins said indignantly. 'What kind of knights do you take us for?'

Lord Errol snorted. 'Highly ignorant ones. We are griffins, not *monsters*!'

'Well, you were banished after the war,' Bronte said.

'Ah yes, they rounded us all up like crumbs and swept us into the kingdoms' dustpan. Their only reason? We chose not to kill other humans at their command. Huh. As if we, the great griffins, would allow ourselves to remain imprisoned.'

Bronte listened with fascination. 'So you haven't been living in the Forgotten Kingdoms then?'

Lord Errol tipped his mighty head. 'Might I remind you, this isn't a pleasant chat over tea. Perhaps we could continue this conversation once I'm free?'

Bronte hesitated.

'You wound me, madam, with your silent accusations! You hurt me with your –'

'OK, fine. *Fine*,' said Bronte before the griffin lord could launch into another rambling protestation. 'Help me get this net off him.'

Reluctantly Tonkins joined Bronte and their firecats in freeing Lord Errol as he huffed and puffed. The knife Blue had found proved to be most useful in cutting through the knots.

'Watch the feathers!' Lord Errol exclaimed, glaring at Dotty, who had one in her mouth. She spat it out and gave the griffin a look of apology. 'I don't suppose you've seen my belongings anywhere?' he asked Bronte.

She wasn't quite sure what belongings a griffin might have. 'Is this knife yours?' she asked. 'It's the only thing we've found.'

'Pfft! What would *I* want with that puny-looking blade?'

Perhaps he realised he'd been a bit rude because moments later, he started making conversation. 'As it happens,' he said, 'the griffins left the Forgotten Kingdoms years ago, though we occasionally return for a visit. No, these days we prefer to make the Vanishing Kingdom our home. No humans.'

'So how did you end up here?' Bronte asked,

eager to learn more.

'I was on patrol. We keep an eye on things because we can't trust humans to be in charge. Not only have they managed to lose the lightning steeds, but the thunder trolls are out of the sky and merrily stomping this way.'

'How far away?' Bronte asked in alarm. 'Are they close to POOP and SICK?'

'The little royals are perfectly safe. The trolls didn't go that way. It is your own skin you should be concerned about. They're coming here – and soon.'

Bronte had the nagging sense that she was missing something obvious. She remembered what Lady Fennel had told her: she should use her head to complete a quest. She screwed her eyes shut, trying to think of everything that seemed wrong.

'The trolls, the *horror*flies, *bad*leys . . .' she murmured out loud.

'What are you muttering about, small human?' Lord Errol asked. 'Pay attention! Careful with that knife!'

'I'm listing every weird thing that's happening round here,' she said, continuing to untie the net. 'There's the endless and unusually bad weather, the gnomes sneaking about –'

'The gnomes?' Tonkins said. 'They're only pinching a few clouds. And running around naked. Which *is* really concerning actually. I mean, no one needs to see that, do they?'

'But why clouds?' Bronte insisted.

Tonkins shrugged. 'Dunno, only the battle boars eat them –'

'No, they're not the only ones . . . That's it!' Bronte exclaimed loudly.

'What is?' Tonkins was confused.

The thought had struck Bronte like lightning itself. 'They're here, in the forest!'

Tonkins stared at her for a moment. '*Who?*'

'The lightning steeds! Think about it, it hasn't just been stormy – there are constant lightning strikes. And you said the gnomes live in the forest, right? Well, who are they giving the clouds *to*? It's got to be the steeds because they also eat clouds. So . . . so maybe they're trapped like Lord Errol here. Possibly even by the same people. Which *finally* explains the thunder trolls. Usually it's the lightning steeds chasing them but now it's the other way round! They're coming here to find the steeds!'

Tonkins frowned. 'Wait, what? I thought you said they were scared of the steeds. Why would they want to find them?'

'They *belong* together! For better or worse, I think the thunder trolls probably can't keep away, even if they want to. You're right, Tonkins, we have to tell the headmaster. We need every knight sweeping the forest until we find the steeds.'

'It doesn't explain the *horror*flies or the *bad*leys though,' Tonkins pointed out.

'No,' Bronte said, her certainty deflating. 'But it *has* to be connected.'

She gave a final tug of the net and at last they managed to pull Lord Errol free.

He stood to full height.

Feathers! He was a lot taller than Bronte had expected, and actually rather scary.

Lord Errol shook himself all over and then dipped his head to look at her. 'Though it gives me no pleasure whatsoever, I am much obliged to you, small human. Forgive me if I don't stay to make more small talk. If you could refrain from telling anybody about this, I would be grateful – I have my reputation to think of. Indeed, I'm not sure how I shall live down being rescued by someone as small as you. Good day, insignificant ones!'

And with that he soared into the air, disappearing above the tops of the trees.

Bronte and Tonkins stared at each other.

'Charming,' Tonkins said, stroking Dotty's head.

The sound of approaching voices made them jump. 'That must be the brothers returning,' Bronte said. 'Run!'

'No time,' Tonkins said. 'Climb!'

They started to scale the nearest tree – Dotty flying and Blue choosing to scramble up the bark.

They had barely hidden themselves when two figures appeared beneath them.

'It's gone!'

'I can see that!'

They lifted the net as if hoping the griffin might somehow still be magically beneath it.

'Ackley's going to be fuming!'

'It would have made such a good weapon. Mutating these animals is one thing, but he still needs something stronger to get past the grim gargoyles.'

Bronte gasped and, in her shock, her grip slipped on the knife and it fell to the forest floor.

One of the men turned around at the sound, and Bronte held her breath, silently begging him not to look up.

'Hol, isn't that your knife?'

'Oh yeah. Must have dropped it before.'

'Never mind that. Look, forget the griffin. We'll catch something else for what Ackley wants. But first we have to find that tree-munching monster that escaped and get it back to base. Got to keep the boss happy, right?'

Gathering up the net in a hurry, the two men scarpered.

Bronte and Tonkins practically fell out of the tree in their hurry to get down.

'That was close!' Tonkins said, hugging Dotty tightly.

'Did you hear them?' Bronte asked. 'They're working for a boss. That's what the gnomes were muttering! It *is* all linked! Come on!'

Useless Knights

Bronte and Tonkins made straight for Sir Blake's tower and ran up the twisty staircase.

When they burst into his office they practically collapsed on the floor, exhausted.

The headmaster was not alone. Lady Fennel was there too, placing a tray of food onto his desk.

She stared at them in shock, while Sir Blake,

who had – unsurprisingly – been napping in his chair, opened his eyes in surprise.

'Goodness gracious me! What is the meaning of this?'

'The forest,' Bronte gasped. 'Bad men.'

'Scary big badley,' Tonkins panted.

'POOP. SICK. *Danger* . . .' Bronte trailed off, unable to talk any more.

'You children make no sense,' Sir Blake said, looking to Lady Fennel, whose expression gave nothing away.

'There are men in the forest, sir,' Tonkins clarified. 'They're doing something, we don't know what, but we think they're doing things to the animals. Growing them. *Mutating* them, sir!'

'They mentioned the grim gargoyles,' Bronte said, having caught her breath. 'I think they're planning some kind of attack on the Realm of Education.'

'And we think the lightning steeds might be in the forest too. With gnomes,' Tonkins said. 'Naked gnomes,' he added, for good measure.

Sir Blake peered at them both over his spectacles, frowning. 'I see.'

Bronte's shoulders sagged. She could tell he didn't believe them. Or worse, he didn't care. Either way, he clearly wasn't interested in helping.

Sir Blake stroked the snoring firecat whose head rested on his knee. 'Well, goodness, haven't you got active imaginations. But I'm far too old for such games. Lady Fennel, would you be kind enough to return these children to wherever they came from? Oh, is this stew? Delicious. Chef does make a splendid dumpling.'

As Lady Fennel started to usher Bronte and Tonkins out of the room, Bronte turned to the teacher she trusted most.

'Please! We have to do something,' she pleaded.

Lady Fennel glanced at Sir Blake before she fixed Bronte with a fierce gaze.

'You went into the forest? On your own? Against explicit orders?'

'No! I mean, yes, but you're missing the point!' Bronte cried in frustration. 'You have to look at the bigger picture!'

'Bronte Tempestra!' Lady Fennel shouted so fiercely that Bronte shrank away. 'The bigger picture is that you have broken school rules.'

'Don't you believe us?' Bronte asked, growing angrier by the minute.

'What I believe is that you have disappointed

me,' she replied. 'And you leave me no choice but to punish you.'

She marched the two disgraced knights out of the room, back down the stairs and all the way to the Calligraphy classroom, where she pointed to the empty ink pots.

'Stay here and refill these. I'll be back once I've spoken with Sir Blake.'

And with one last devastating glare, Lady Fennel left the room.

'We're going back,' Bronte said once she was gone.

Tonkins stared at her in horror. 'To the *forest*? Bronte, we're *literally* being punished for having just done that!'

'If we don't, those men are going to attack POOP and SICK! What is the point of knights if they don't defend those who need defending?'

'We're NINE!' Tonkins shouted at her. 'We're not knights! You've been here less than a week. You can't even ride a battle boar!'

Bronte's temper flared scarlet. 'I fell off ONCE! And what does that have to do with anything? At least I'm not too scared to go into a forest!'

'Well, sorry if I want to stay alive!' Tonkins was equally furious now. 'Being reckless doesn't make you brave, Bronte.'

'What about the lightning steeds? Don't you at least want to try and find them? Before the thunder trolls arrive and stampede us all? To *DEATH!*'

'You don't even know for certain that they will.'

'Stay here then, fill up stupid ink pots. I am not going to be a *useless* knight!'

'You are SO getting kicked out!' Tonkins shouted after her as she stormed out of the classroom.

Bronte fought back the tears threatening to spill. The last thing she wanted was to fight with Tonkins, but this was something she had to do. Taking a deep breath, she scanned the courtyard to see if the coast was clear. 'OK, come on, Blue, keep up.'

The firekitten seemed to take that as an invitation to leap onto Bronte's head and perch there like an uncomfortable hat.

'We have to find out how those men are turning the animals into monsters – and what exactly they're planning,' whispered Bronte as they skulked through the school grounds. 'I'm certain the lightning steeds have something to do with this. They must be in the forest and we have to save them – before the thunder trolls turn up and destroy everything!'

Back at the edge of the forest, Bronte's anger was replaced immediately with regret as she was reminded of just how scary the woodland was.

She wished Tonkins was here. Right now she particularly missed the sound of his voice chattering away beside her.

As if sensing her fear, Blue nuzzled close to Bronte.

Taking a deep breath, Bronte grabbed a large

stick from the ground and held it up like a sword as she edged her way through the dense foliage.

The wind raged and the trees creaked in the storm. The rain tapped endlessly on the leaves and dripped down her nose. But then a different sound made her freeze. Something was out there.

Blue growled and tried once more to breathe fire. But again, he only managed a few puffs of air.

'Don't worry, Blue, I'll protect you,' Bronte said, pretending she didn't notice her voice shaking with fear.

The trees rustled, the sounds getting louder and louder until . . . Tonkins came hurtling through the branches, with Dotty right behind him.

'Tonkins?!' Bronte cried, in sheer relief.

'I could hardly let you come in here alone, could I?' he said, looking a little sheepish.

Bronte gave him a huge hug. 'Thank you. And I'm sorry.'

'I'm sorry too, I should have come in the first place.' Tonkins looked around. 'Curly custard, the forest seems even creepier than before, which I did *not* think was possible.'

'And it's getting dark – we need to get a move on.'

'What are we looking for anyway?'

'Any signs that the lightning steeds are here,' Bronte said.

'Like tracks?'

'Yup. And you'll spot these ones easily. The steeds rarely come to ground but, when they do, they leave scorch marks behind.'

'OK, burn marks in the ground, got it. Exactly what you want to see in a place full of things that can catch fire.'

They hurried as fast as they could, scanning the damp forest floor, but as time passed Bronte began to fear they would never find anything. If someone wanted to hide, this would be the perfect place to do it.

'Hey, look!'

Bronte did as she was told and smiled. 'It's a nibbit!'

'And it actually looks like one,' Tonkins said in relief.

Bronte, temporarily distracted, slowly walked towards the little animal and stretched her fingers out to beckon it over. 'It's so cute – here, little nib— **AARGGH!**'

In a blink of an eye, the 'cute' nibbit's mouth flew open so wide that its whole head seemed to grow, revealing massive fangs, dripping with blood and snapping at Bronte's outstretched

hand. She only just kept her fingers!

'Why is this happening to me?' Tonkins screamed, as he and Bronte fled.

The mutant zombie nibbit gave chase and was soon joined by several more of the ravenous creatures.

'Of all the ways I thought I'd die, being eaten by *zombits* was not one of them!' Tonkins shrieked as they struggled to keep ahead of the swarm hopping behind them. Several times Dotty paused in flight to blast them with flames. Even though it slowed them down, it didn't stop them entirely.

'Maybe we should climb a tree again? Can they climb?' Bronte shouted.

'How should I know?! We never covered

zombits in class! Just keep going, and make sure you don't trip over anything or –'

He never finished his sentence because he was so busy looking at Bronte that he didn't notice the branch ahead of him, and smashed right into it, knocking himself out cold and dropping to the forest floor.

'Tonkins? Tonkins!' Bronte rushed to his side, but he didn't move.

The zombits were getting ever closer as she tried to lift Tonkins up. It was no use, he was all floppy.

'Come on, Tonkins. Wake up!' she shouted. '*Please!*' She could almost hear the zombits' gnashing teeth now.

Desperation had her in its grip when a great shadow fell over them.

She looked up and there, beside her, now

dressed in top hat, bow tie and monocle, was . . .

'Lord Errol!' Bronte cried.

'It would appear you are in need of assistance, small humans,' the griffin said. And he stretched out his wings, wrapping one around Tonkins and the other around Bronte, before lifting them onto his back.

'Off we go then!' he bellowed, and set off at a gallop through the trees.

Deadly Dangers

Lord Errol soon outran the flesh-eating *zombits* and, once the danger was past, came to a halt.

Tonkins was still unconscious, slumped comfortably against Lord Errol's neck. Taking care not to disturb him, Bronte slid to the ground and had to stop herself from hugging the griffin. She didn't think he'd like that much.

'Lord Errol, thank you! You saved us!'

'I simply owed you a debt. Which I have now repaid.'

Bronte looked around, alarmed. 'Where's Blue and Dotty?'

As if she'd heard her, Dotty came flying into view, Blue perched on her back, and landed next to Tonkins, licking his sleeping face in concern.

'I'm so glad you're safe,' Bronte said, scratching Dotty under her chin, and Blue behind his horns.

Blue leaped from Dotty to Bronte's shoulder, digging in his sharp claws to anchor himself.

Lord Errol cleared his throat. 'Well, if you'll excuse me, I must be on my way. Things to do, you know. Could you kindly remove this heavy lump of human from my back?'

'Wait,' Bronte said. 'We still need your help.'

'Small human, I am *not* your ally.'

'And yet here you are. I thought you wanted to get away once you were free?'

'Well, yes, I . . . ah, ahem, well. I had to find my hat and such, you understand. And . . . well . . .' Lord Errol blustered.

'Yes?' Bronte raised an amused eyebrow.

'All *right*, I wanted to make sure you were unscathed, small human. Didn't want those dastardly fellows to catch you too, not on my account. But I swear, if you ever reveal that to another breathing soul, I shall never speak to you again.'

'I promise your secret is safe with me, but please take Tonkins back to the school. He needs help.'

'I'm sorry, it sounded like you just asked me to carry the cowardly one back to a place crawling with humans?'

'I wouldn't ask if I wasn't desperate.'

Lord Errol narrowed his eyes suspiciously. 'And why is that? In fact, *why* are you still in this forest?'

'Those men. They're plotting an attack on the Realm of Education, and I have to stop them. I think they, or whoever they work for, are the ones turning all these poor animals into monsters to create a weird mutant army! Plus I'm sure they're holding the lightning steeds captive.'

Lord Errol stared at her for a moment. 'Why should *you* care about any of that?'

'My family, my friends, my *home*. They're all in danger. I haven't heard anything from my parents since I arrived and I don't know if they're OK.' Bronte hesitated before adding, 'And because I'm a knight. That's what we do. Defend those that need defending. Sir Pen Tine taught me that, even if the school doesn't seem to want to.'

Again, Lord Errol considered her. 'What is your name, small human?'

'Bronte Tempestra of –'

'Of the Storm Kingdom?' he interrupted, and then paused. 'It may relieve you to learn that the castle still stands in your kingdom. I've heard nothing to suggest you need be alarmed for your family.'

'Really? Thank you!' It was a relief to hear that, but there were too many other pressing problems for her to relax for long.

Lord Errol straightened his bow tie with his front hoof. 'Very well, small human. I shall honour your request and take your cowardly companion as far as the edge of the forest, but after that, his firecat will have to raise the alarm.'

'Thank you,' Bronte said, again wishing she could hug him.

Lord Errol sighed dramatically. 'Honestly, you humans! So weak, so pathetic. How I lower myself to become nothing more than a steed for an incompetent knight. I will return when I've done your bidding to help you catch your villains. I have my own score to settle.'

Bronte nodded and squeezed Tonkins's hand goodbye. 'Be quick,' she said.

Lord Errol pulled a face and, wrapping his wings across his back to stop Tonkins from falling, took off at a gallop towards the school, Dotty speeding behind him.

For a few moments, Bronte stood still, not

quite knowing what to do. It suddenly all seemed so overwhelming, until –

A low growl sounded behind her and Bronte froze. Slowly she turned around to find herself staring up at a giant squibble. Its bushy green tail was filled with glinting blades, sharper than any sword. And it was angry. Very angry.

'Nice squibble,' Bronte said, stepping slowly back.

In response it swished its tail, shooting its blades right at her!

Immediately Bronte leaped and twisted to avoid being hit. 'Not a nice squibble, an evil squibble! A squevil!'

Bronte ran fast, not waiting for a second attack, when a lightning bolt blazed right in front of her, hitting a tree and setting it alight!

'The steeds must be close! If we find them, maybe we'll find Elon and Hollis and stop them doing whatever it is they're doing before they can do whatever it is they're planning to do to POOP and SICK!' She frowned, realising how little she actually knew, but shook the thought away. Now wasn't the time for doubts. 'This way, Blue!'

Another bolt struck, and another, as if guiding her way. But then, with a sinking heart, Bronte realised something else too. The ground was shaking with a familiar thud.

'Oh no!' she cried. In all the drama she'd almost forgotten the other threat facing them. 'The thunder trolls are nearly here. Hurry!'

They ran as fast as they could, but then they rounded a corner and came to an abrupt halt.

The way was blocked!

Three massive twelve-legged beasts were swinging from the trees, one behind the other, all dangling from a thick rope and gnashing their teeth. They looked a bit like the spiddlers Bronte had read about in her text book, apart from the fact that spiddlers were usually the size of her fingertip and completely harmless! Beyond them was a *badley*, who was snacking on a fallen log and looking most upset to be nearly finished.

Bronte stared at the sight before her. There was something eerily familiar about it.

'It's just like the gauntlet run!' she said to herself, not wanting to remember how badly that had gone. But as more lightning struck, as the ground juddered violently and the storm grew wilder, she knew she had no choice. She had to at least try to get past.

She waited for the first humongous spiddler

to swing high to the right and then ran, Blue clinging tightly to her shoulders. Halting abruptly, she paused for the next one to make its pendulum swing, then dashed forward, before sprinting past the final nasty forest mutation.

'Yes!'

But her celebration quickly ended. The *badley* opened its massive jaw in a roar. Clearly Bronte looked like a good extra snack. Blue leaped from Bronte's shoulder and onto the *badley*'s nose, where he proceeded to scratch the creature's snout with his needle-like claws.

It gave Bronte the distraction she needed, and she rolled right through the *badley*'s legs. Unlike in the classroom, this time she created enough momentum to safely make it out the other side.

Only to come face to face with a pack of fixels! Bronte knew from the classroom posters that they had sharp teeth, but the flames that replaced their fur were unexpected.

They growled and started to edge towards Bronte.

Before Bronte could think of a plan, Blue came leaping down from the *bad*ley and growled as he approached the flaming fixels.

'Blue!' Bronte cried. 'Stop!'

But the firekitten paid her no attention. He crouched low, eyeing up his enemy, and then he blew. And sure enough, it wasn't his usual empty puff that came out. But nor was it fire.

It was ice!

The freezing water sprayed all over the flaming fixels, putting out their fiery backs until they were shivering and yelping.

'You're an *ice*kitten!' Bronte exclaimed in delight. 'Breezy!'

But in her dash past the now cowering fixels, Bronte slipped on the ice. Sliding and skidding, she screamed as she flew along, until the ground fell away and then suddenly she was falling, tumbling down until she landed with a **THUMP**.

An Evil Scientist

'Ow,' Bronte moaned as she sat up. Blue licked her face as if to apologise. 'Where are we?'

They had fallen into a valley and in front of them were the remains of an ancient castle. It had been consumed by the forest – covered in moss and ivy, with anything and everything green twisting around it.

'A perfect hiding place?' Bronte asked Blue.

They crept towards the crumbling building where they found an arched doorway – minus the door.

As they edged further inside, a strange noise reached their ears – a great churning, whirring sound.

'What the green gravy?' Bronte asked, looking at Blue.

As they crept on cautiously, the noise grew louder and soon became accompanied by others. Crackling, buzzing. *Voices*.

They walked up a narrow spiral staircase and found themselves in an old viewing gallery, looking down on what had once been, long ago, a great hall.

Now the room was full of strange machines, some pumping water, others chugging and grinding, and *sparking*. And there were lots of gnomes running busily all over the place, each clearly with a job to do. As Bronte took it all in, she noticed an animal strapped to a table in the centre, hooked up to numerous wires.

Wait, was that . . . *Pig*?!

The wires ran the length of the hall, into the many machines. The largest had several coming out of the other end and Bronte's eyes followed where they led. She gasped!

The lightning steeds!

Inside the metal barred pen, they were hardly recognisable. The legendary reds and oranges that Bronte knew usually flickered brightly through their manes and tails were now muted, their once shiny black coats now a dull grey.

Who in the curly custard was doing all this?

As if answering her unspoken question, a loud voice boomed through the air, making Bronte jump.

'Are you ready yet?'

Walking into the hall was a man with shaggy brown hair held back by a pair of goggles on top of his head. He had little circular glasses at the end of his long nose, and his clothes were splodged with what looked like burn marks.

The gnomes cowered in his presence and worked faster.

'What,' the man said, walking towards Pig, 'is that?'

'A battle boar, Mr Ackley, sir, just as you asked.'

The man lifted the gnome from the ground.

'That,' and he pointed angrily at Pig, 'is no battle boar.'

'Sorry, Mr Ackley, sir, we took him from the pens just like you said.'

Ackley practically threw the gnome back onto the ground. 'Idiots! You're as bad as Elon and

Hollis! I should never have trusted them after they set the mutated forrerflies on the school for squires rather than the Realm of Education. What use is a practice run if you attack the wrong place? I'm surrounded by incompetence!'

Another gnome crept up timidly. 'The machines are ready, sir.'

Ackley wandered over and studied Pig. 'I needed tusks! If I'm to avenge the Tree Kingdoms and reclaim my birth right as King of the Oak Kingdom, the first thing I need to do is destroy the royal schools. And in order to get past the grim gargoyles, I need to mutate the tusks of battle boars into diamond. Nothing else can cut through the stone guardians. This pathetic excuse for a boar is not what I need. Now I'll have to change my calculations!'

Bronte looked at Blue in shock. This was

about the *Tree Kingdoms*? She hadn't seen that coming! So that's why he wanted to attack POOP and SICK. He was planning to overthrow the Realm of Education and restore it to the old Oak Kingdom!

Ackley walked to the biggest machine, pressing buttons and pulling levers, sending lightning flashing out. The steeds trembled in their pen, as if they knew what was coming.

'Now!' Ackley barked, and gnomes wearing oven gloves ran up to the metal pen.

Bronte watched in horror as they poked the lightning steeds with sharp prods. Lightning shot from the horses' hooves in their fear and pain. It struck the metal bars, travelling with a loud crackle down the wires and into Ackley's machine. It shuddered and shook and then Ackley pulled the biggest lever, sending the lightning hissing and growling down the wires and into Pig, who squealed, painfully, loudly.

Bronte had no love for the pigling who'd dumped her in a pile of poop, but this was awful. She feared the lightning would surely kill him, but instead he started to grow, larger and larger, until he was far bigger than a fully-grown battle boar. Sharp tusks burst through his skin, dazzling like diamonds, and his bottom teeth protruded like blades. His tufts of fur were singed by the heat and sparks of lightning were coming from his skin.

'Yes!' Ackley cried triumphantly. 'YES! A weapon strong enough to cut through stone! Once we steal the rest of the battle boars and transform them, we'll be unstoppable!'

It all made sense at last. The gnomes were stealing clouds to feed the lightning steeds, which

Ackley had stolen in order to run his evil machine with their lightning, which he was using to turn innocent animals into mutant weapons. All so he could seize control of the old Oak Kingdom. And what then? Would he want to reclaim the other Tree Kingdoms too?

This was precisely the kind of thing Sir Pen Tine wouldn't stand for – and neither would Bronte.

'We need to destroy that machine,' Bronte whispered to Blue.

She waited until Ackley's back was turned and then carefully stepped over the ledge to climb down the wall.

When she reached the great hall, she ran low to hide behind an old barrel. She had to figure out a way to get to the machine unnoticed.

But as she sat there, formulating her plan, a

gnome suddenly appeared before her, clipboard in hand. He stared back at her and they both froze. Then Bronte raised her finger to her lips, hoping to convince the gnome not to give her away.

For a moment, she thought it might work. And then the gnome began screaming, running about wildly, waving his oven-mitted hands in the air and pointing in her direction.

Bronte looked around in alarm.

All the other gnomes started dashing frantically around too, their screams drowning out all other noise, their arms flailing in the air, their little bottoms flashing.

'What the . . . ?' Ackley exclaimed.

Bronte made a dash towards the machine, taking advantage of the chaos, but Ackley saw her and quickly ran to intercept her.

'Blue, ice him!'

The icekitten swooped and blasted the ground, so that Ackley skidded and slipped before crashing down.

Bronte made it to the machine. She searched among all the levers and buttons until she found a lever labelled *off*. She pulled it.

Instantly the machine stopped and Pig ceased squealing, though he still grunted and strained at his straps.

Ackley was staggering back to his feet now.

'How did you get in here? You're meddling

in things that do not concern you, little girl,' he said, snatching up a spanner and holding it out like a weapon.

'They most certainly do! You'll never attack POOP and SICK, you'll never take over the Realm of Education!'

'Poop? Sick? What are you talking about?' Ackley sounded confused. Then he shook his head. 'Never mind. You may have discovered what I'm doing, but it'll be impossible for you to tell anyone when you're my prisoner. Minions!'

The gnomes swarmed towards her, despite Blue hissing fiercely at them.

'Leave him alone!' Bronte cried, as Ackley reached out to grab Blue.

'Your icekitten will make a tremendous addition to my army,' Ackley said. 'And as for you? Well, you can be the first test subject for part two of my plan – transforming people into obedient soldiers. Tie her up!'

The gnomes started to wrap rope around Bronte as she struggled desperately. This was all going very wrong!

'Excuse me, but I must insist you let the small human go.'

Bronte grinned widely with relief. 'Lord Errol!'

'What the –' Ackley spluttered.

'You see,' Lord Errol continued, 'the only reason I haven't eaten you already is because she would disapprove of me doing so. But continue to hold her prisoner and she might well change her mind.'

'You can't hurt me,' Ackley said, though for the first time he sounded unsure. He turned to Bronte. 'Without me, you can never undo what's been done. The pigling will stay beastly, and your kingdoms will be filled with murderous woodland animals. You need me!'

In all the commotion, the gnomes had loosened their grip on the rope. Bronte shrugged it off and ran back to the machine.

'Oh yeah? What about this lever here? The one labelled *reverse*?'

Ackley's face fell. 'Oh. I didn't know you'd seen that. Noooo!' he cried, as Bronte pulled it.

The machine started to whir and whine again, but this time, the lightning travelled back the other way. The machine sucked it out of Pig, whose body started to shrink to its normal size, his teeth returning into his mouth, until eventually he was exactly the same as he had been before – all apart from the diamond tusks, which didn't move an inch.

Ackley ran towards Bronte, his spanner raised.

Lord Errol didn't hesitate and stormed after him, kicking the scientist in the head. Ackley fell to the ground with a thud.

The gnomes stared at the body on the floor and started to scream again, fleeing the room as fast as they could.

Bronte ran over to join Lord Errol. This time she couldn't resist hugging him. 'Thank you!'

Lord Errol nodded his head in gratitude, before nudging Ackley's body with his hoof. 'He'll have a splitting headache when he wakes.'

'What are we going to do with him?' Bronte asked. 'Take him back to the school?'

'No need,' Lord Errol said. 'I suspect those he's wronged might wish to deal with him.' And he glanced towards the steeds huddled in the pen.

Bronte ran over to the gate and rattled the padlock. 'How am I going to get them out?'

'Maybe Dotty can help?' a familiar voice said, and Bronte looked up to see Tonkins sitting on a fierce battle boar with black fur. Behind him was Lady Fennel, her sword drawn. Dotty and Shadow flew beside them.

'You're OK!' Bronte cried out as Lady Fennel took in the chaos.

'Young Tonkins woke up moments after Dotty led me to him,' she said. 'He told me where you were and we came to rescue you. I can see that wasn't entirely necessary.'

'Thundering hooves,' Lord Errol sighed. 'There are three too many humans in this room for my liking. I believe it's time for me to leave.' He bowed before Bronte. 'It has been . . . an experience, small human. One I shall not forget, though goodness knows I shall try. To be reminded that I allowed myself not only to associate with one such as yourself, but that I also experienced the mildest hint of admiration for you, is possibly more than I can endure. Truly, the likes of me, a griffin lord, consorting with fragile two-legged people, oh it –'

'I'll miss you too,' Bronte said with a grin.

'Is he always like this?' Lady Fennel asked, bemused.

'Always,' Tonkins confirmed with a groan.

'At least I didn't knock myself out on a twig,' the griffin shot back with a glare, before adding more gently, 'though I am glad you are not dead, little cowardly one.'

'Er . . . thanks?' Tonkins looked at Bronte who laughed.

'Farewell!' And Lord Errol flew off back the way that Bronte had come in.

'Tempestra, who is that man lying on the floor?' Lady Fennel asked, still looking around in shock. 'And why does Pig have sparkling tusks? And oh my, are they the lightning steeds?'

'It's a long story. But first, can you help me set them free?'

'Dotty, see what you can do,' Tonkins said.

The firecat flew over, joined by Shadow, and the two of them blew fire together, melting the lock away so that Bronte could open the pen and release the lightning steeds.

As they trotted out, Bronte gazed at the sight before her. It was very rare that anyone living on land was fortunate enough to get so close to these magnificent beings. Though their ordeal had drained much of their radiance, Bronte was still enchanted.

The leader of the herd came over to Ackley and looked down on him with disgust. Some of the other horses fetched one of the cloud nets from the corner of the room, and then dropped it over his body. They scooped him up and, pausing briefly to nod their thanks to the group, they stormed out of the building.

Bronte, Tonkins and Lady Fennel ran outside to watch the steeds go.

There in the night sky, galloping and prancing among the stars, were the lightning steeds, their colours returning to their former glory with every passing moment. Suspended below the magnificent horses, still trapped in the net they carried, was Ackley and Bronte could hear his cries for help even at such a distance. With a final chorus of whinnies, the horses turned for home, towards the Storm Kingdom, taking Ackley with them.

And then they were gone.

A Moment's Peace

Lady Fennel's arms were wrapped around Bronte, holding her steady on the battle boar as they journeyed back through the forest to Sir Sebastian's. Tonkins lay on Shadow's back, fast asleep, while Dotty and Blue played together – Dotty breathing fire and Blue quickly putting it out with his ice.

'I'm sorry, Bronte,' Lady Fennel said in the

stillness of the night. 'I did believe you, but I wanted to keep you from any danger. I've suspected since those giant forrerflies attacked that something strange was happening in the forest, but I wasn't sure who I could trust. I sensed whoever was up to no good was being helped by someone at the school. At first I thought Lampton was the culprit.'

'It wasn't him?'

'No,' said Lady Fennel grimly. 'It was Sir Blake.'

'What?!'

'In his defence, he didn't know exactly what was going on. He simply didn't refuse Ackley's request to privately hire the forest, and then kept his presence from the rest of us.'

'What will happen now?' Bronte asked.

'Sir Calliphus will take over as headmaster, for now at least. And once I've returned you two safely back to school, I won't rest until all the animals have been through the reversal machine. I think it will have enough lightning power left from Pig to run even without the steeds. Then I'll dismantle the equipment so that it can never be used to cause harm again.'

'What about Ackley's brothers?'

'Don't worry, I suspect they're long gone. But I'll keep an eye out while I'm making the forest safe again.'

When they reached the triple-trunk oak, Bronte slid off the battle boar and smiled up at Lady Fennel.

'Thank you,' she said.

'Thank *you*. You're turning into quite the formidable knight. Now get some rest. I'll make sure Tonkins here gets to bed.'

Bronte was very tired as she climbed up

the ladder into her cabin. Blue snorted some snowflakes before he fell instantly asleep beneath Bronte's hammock. Bronte flopped inside it, and pulled her Sir Pen Tine toy to her chest. It didn't matter if he wasn't real, if he was just made up. The legend was real to her and that was what counted.

Content, but exhausted, she was just wondering whether she could be bothered to put her pyjamas on, when there was a tap on the door.

Wearily, she tiptoed over and opened it.

'Lord Errol!'

The griffin lord's powerful wings kept him still in the sky outside her treehouse and he tipped his top hat to her.

'Good evening, small human, may I come in?' he asked, before squeezing past her into the room. 'Forgive my intrusion, but I wished to convey news that I believe will be of interest to you.'

'Did the steeds make it safely home?' Bronte asked.

'They did indeed. More importantly, they made quick work of rounding up the thunder trolls, who are now all returned to the sky in your kingdom where they belong. And I think it'll please you to hear that they have some new entertainment. A certain wild-haired scientist will spend his days being chased through the skies, if he doesn't wish to be trodden on by clumsy-footed giant trolls.'

Bronte gasped with surprise. 'The horses left Ackley up in the sky?'

'Yes, a rather fitting punishment for the man who dared to steal them, don't you think?'

Bronte almost felt sorry for Ackley. Almost.

'The kingdoms are safe once more, thanks to you,' Lord Errol said. 'I must say, you have impressed me.'

Bronte blushed. There was no higher compliment.

'Can I ask you something? Ackley said he was avenging the Tree Kingdoms, that he should have been King of the Oak Kingdom. Do you think that was true?'

Lord Errol nodded. 'I believe it was.'

'Then surely he won't give up so easily? If he's been plotting all this time? What if he escapes the Storm Kingdom?'

'I think that task is beyond him alone.'

'But he has two brothers.'

'Buffoons. Do not worry yourself,' Lord Errol said. 'Now, you need your rest. After all, the next quest is surely just around the corner.' And he lifted his monocle from his eye to wink at her.

When he was gone, Bronte stared out across the school grounds, past the trees and into the distance beyond. A whole world yet to be explored.

Yes, she thought to herself. The next quest. Maybe that would be another adventure, or maybe it would just be surviving school. But whatever happened, she knew she could handle it.

She was, after all, a knight.

SIR SEBASTIAN'S SCHOOL FOR SQUIRES

Set in the Heart of the Kingdoms, surrounded by beautiful woodland, is our prestigious establishment – we welcome you to come and join the historic tradition of Knighthood.

- Learn from the best jousting champions.

- Discover how to become a *HERO*.

- Quills of the finest plumage.

OPEN FOR THE FIRST TIME TO ALL STUDENTS.

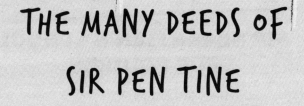

THE MANY DEEDS OF
SIR PEN TINE

A YEAR 3 PRODUCTION

CAST:

Sir Pen Tine — Bronte Tempestra
Firkle — Mariam Haze
Hurkle — Fleur Tendril
The Swirklebirkle — Skye Aura &
Posy Thorne
The Princess Belle — Eliane Blaze
Christopher Farron — Ailla Green
Mo, the Weather Witch — Enya Ember

Sir Pen Tine and his firecat, Firkle
Went to slay the Swirklebirkle
And with the battle boar (name of Hurkle)
They trapped the beast inside a circle.
CHARGE!
FIRE!
SWORD!
And that's how Sir Pen Tine and Firkle
(And don't forget their brave steed Hurkle)
Slew the mighty Swirklebirkle

Weather Witch Mo turned the whole world to snow
Firkle breathed fire and made it all go
The wicked witch thwarted
Her mess fixed and sorted
Sir Pen Tine's firecat was a hero!

The foul robber baron
Bad Christopher Faron
Kidnapped the Princess Belle
Sir Pen Tine came riding
To give him a hiding
And rescue the Princess as well.

Piccadilly

PRESS

We hope you loved your Piccadilly Press book!

For all the latest bookish news, freebies and exclusive
content, sign up to the Piccadilly Press newsletter –
scan the QR code or visit lnk.to/PiccadillyNewsletter

Follow us on social media:

bonnierbooks.co.uk/PiccadillyPress